The Dorset Boy – Lady Bethany – Gr

This is a work of Fiction. All characters and stories are fictional although based in historical settings. If you see your name appear in the story, it is a coincidence, or maybe I asked first.

Acknowledgements

Thanks to Dawn Spears the brilliant artist who created the cover artwork and my editor Debz Hobbs-Wyatt without whom the books wouldn't be as good as they are.

My wife who is so supportive and believes in me. Last my dogs Blaez and Zeeva and cats Vaskr and Rosa who watch me act out the fight scenes and must wonder what the hell has gotten into their boss. And a special thank you to Troy who was the grandfather of Blaez in real life. He was a magnificent beast just like his grandson!

THANK YOU FOR READING!

I hope you enjoy reading this book as much as I enjoyed writing it. Reviews are so helpful to authors. I really appreciate all reviews, both positive and negative. If you want to leave one, you can do so on Amazon, through my website, or on Twitter.

About the Author

Christopher C Tubbs is a dog-loving descendent of a long line of Dorset clay miners and has chased his family tree back to the 16th century in the Isle of Purbeck. He left school at sixteen to train as an Avionics Craftsman, has been a public speaker at conferences for most of his career and was one of the founders of a successful games company back in the 1990s. Now in his sixties, he finally writes the stories he had been dreaming about for years. Thanks to inspiration from great authors like Alexander Kent, Dewey Lambdin, Patrick O'Brian, Raymond E Feist, and Dudley Pope, he was finally able to put digit to keyboard. He lives in the Netherlands Antilles with his wife, two Dutch Shepherds, and two Norwegian Forest cats.

You can visit him on his website
www.thedorsetboy.com
The Dorset Boy, Facebook page.

Or tweet him @ChristopherCTu3

The Dorset Boy Series Timeline

1792 – 1795   Book 1: A Talent for Trouble
Marty joins the navy as an assistant steward and through a series of adventures ends up a midshipman.

1795 – 1798   Book 2: The Special Operations Flotilla
Marty is a founder member of the Special Operations Flotilla, learns to be a spy and passes as Lieutenant.

1799 – 1802   Book 3: Agent Provocateur
Marty teams up with Linette to infiltrate Paris, marries Caroline, becomes a father and fights pirates in Madagascar.

1802 – 1804   Book 4: In Dangerous Company
Marty and Caroline are in India helping out Arthur Wellesley, combatting French efforts to disrupt the East India Company and French-sponsored pirates on Reunion. James Stockley born.

1804 – 1805   Book 5: The Tempest
Piracy in the Caribbean, French interference, Spanish gold and the death of Nelson. Marty makes Captain.

1806 – 1807   Book 6: Vendetta
A favour carried out for a prince, a new ship, the S.O.F. move to Gibraltar, the battle of Maida, counter espionage in Malta and a Vendetta declared and closed.

1807 – 1809   Book 7: The Trojan Horse
Rescue of the Portuguese royal family, Battle of the Basque Roads with Thomas Cochrane, and back to the Indian Ocean and another conflict with the French Intelligence Service.

1809 – 1811   Book 8: La Licorne
Marty takes on the role of Viscount Wellington's Head of Intelligence. Battle of The Lines of Torres Vedras, siege of Cadiz, skulduggery, espionage and blowing stuff up to confound the French.

1812   Book 9: Raider
Marty is busy. From London to Paris to America and back to the Mediterranean for the battle of Salamanca. A mission to the Adriatic reveals a white-slavery racket that results in a private mission to the Caribbean to rescue his children.

1813 – 1814   Book 10: Silverthorn
Promoted to Commodore and given a viscountcy, Marty is sent to the Caribbean to be Governor of Aruba which provides the cover story he needs to fight American privateers and undermine the Spanish in South America. On his return he escorts Napoleon into Exile on Alba.

1815 – 1816   Book 11: Exile
After 100 days in exile Napoleon returns to France and Marty tries to hunt him down. After the battle of Waterloo Marty again escorts him into Exile on St Helena. His help is requested by the Governor of Ceylon against the rebels in Kandy.

1817 – 1818   Book 12: Dynasty
To Paris to stop an assassination, then the Mediterranean to further British interests in the region. Finally, to Calcutta as Military Attaché to take part in the war with the Maratha Empire. Beth comes into her own as a spy, but James prefers the navy life.

1818 -- 1819   Book 13: Empire
The end of the third Anglo-Maratha war and the establishment of the Raj. Intrigue in India, war with the Pindaris, the foundation of Singapore, shipwreck, sea wars and storms.

1820 - 1821   Book 14: Revolution
The Ottoman Empire is starting to disintegrate. The Greeks are starting to revolt. Marty has a promise to keep so Britain can gain Cyprus. Just to complicate things King John of Portugal needs his support as well.

Contents

Spy School

The academy was a stately home in Coleshill, a village in the county of Berkshire. It was designed by Inigo Jones in the 17th century and was a mixture of Dutch, Greek, French and English architecture. It was perfect for training agents as it was secluded and owned by Baron Pleydell-Bouverie whose seat was at Longford Castle in Wiltshire, meaning he had little use for it. Being friends with George Canning it was natural for him to make the house available for the academy.

It had ample bedrooms, bathrooms and reception rooms. The boys slept in dormitories and the lone girl had a room and bathroom to herself. There was an extensive staff, an excellent cook who also taught poisons, and instructors for everything from assassination to surveillance. The grounds were constantly patrolled by 'gamekeepers' armed with shotguns.

The Right Honourable Bethany Stockley, Beth to her friends, codename Chaton (Kitten), was bored. The class was about surveillance and the teacher was a windy old fart who went by the codename Astral. He was expounding on the principles of the quadruple tail, and she had drifted off remembering her time in India. There were only five people in her class and all the others were boys.

"Chaton," Astral said, looking at her over his half-moon glasses. "Would you be so kind as to explain how you would set up a quadruple tail on two men walking through Covent Garden in London."

"Which road will they approach the market from?" Beth said sweetly.

"Does it make a difference?"

"Yes, Sir, it does. If they are coming up from the Strand through the lanes, which are run by the Bow Street gang, it will require one man ahead, two alternating behind and the fourth on the rooftops until they come out into the market proper. Then they can adopt a more traditional one ahead, one behind and one either side formation. But having said that, in a crowded marketplace I would prefer to have a bigger team disguised as porters and buyers who could switch the tail more frequently.

If, however, the mark is approaching from St Martin's, the streets are wider which would allow one ahead, two alternating behind and one across the road."

Beth was about to continue but Astral stopped her.

"That will do nicely, thank you." There was a soft snigger behind her. The end of the class came and Astral stopped her on the way out.

"A moment please, Chaton." Only codenames were used.

"Yes, Mr Astral?" she said innocently.

"I know these classes must seem tedious to you as your esteemed father must have taught you everything, but for the sake of your less privileged colleagues, please try to at least pretend to be interested."

"Sorry, Sir. I will," she said, giving him a curtsy. Her father was the head of the Foreign Division Mobile Unit and their most senior agent. Commodore Lord Martin Stockley of Purbeck, was known variously as Marty, Martin and Boss to his special operations team the Shadows, but known as M internally. As far as Beth knew he never used the code name and would only sign letters as M if they were to his boss Admiral Turner.

The next class was more fun. It was sabotage and involved a fair amount of hands-on activity. She entered the room and realised she was the last to arrive. It was noted by their instructor, Bomber, with a pointed look as he called the class to order.

"Today's subject is bridges. How to cross them without falling off." The class laughed at his joke.

"There are many types of bridges, and they all need a different methodology if you want to take them down." He uncovered a large picture on an easel.

"These are different types of arch bridge. Note the thickness of the pillars and buttresses in each type."

A second picture showed trestle bridges and a third, the latest innovation, the cantilever bridge.

"Now can anybody tell me where the common weak point is on all these arched bridges?"

Hands went up and he chose Brindle. A nondescript boy with a Newcastle accent.

"The centre of the arch, Sir. If one was to blow out the keystone the arch would lose its integrity and collapse."

"Quite right, but what is the disadvantage of that?"

Beth put her hand up.

"Chaton?"

"Easily repaired by laying timbers across the gap."

"Correct. Collapsing the top part of an arch only makes a narrow gap leaving the piers and some of the road intact. So where should you attack this bridge to destroy it?"

Beth assumed he was still talking to her as he was looking in her direction. "As low down the central pier or piers as possible if it has more than one arch. Or set charges in more than one place if it's a single span to make the gap as wide as possible."

"Excellent! Now someone else tell me how the charges should be set," Bomber said.

Beth listened, blowing stuff up was fun. In fact, anything that could go bang was fun in her mind. The theory was only half the class, which lasted all afternoon, the practical part was carried out on large-scale models of bridges in the grounds the school was housed in. The charges used were proportionate and a small army of craftsmen rebuilt the models after every class.

Beth got a trestle bridge. It was made of a latticework of wood and was thirty-feet high with a rail track along the top. This meant she had to climb to set her charges in the right place. Luckily, she had chosen to wear culottes, loose trousers that looked like a skirt which preserved her modesty. She put the satchel that contained her charges over her shoulder and made sure she had the reel of fast fuse coiled nicely. She also carried a length of slower fuse wrapped around her waist.

She started to climb. The two-by-four timbers carried her seven stones of weight without a problem. Beth was agile, a dancer, a gymnast and an expert climber. She had been trained by Chin, a former imperial guard of the Chinese Emperor turned Shadow as part of her father's team, in the art of Qinggong since she could run, and used all her skills to go up the trestle like a spider.

She set her first charge and pushed the end of the fast fuse in it, looping it around a stanchion in a clove hitch to prevent it from being dislodged. She moved on to the next point where she wanted to set a charge, allowing the fast fuse to run out freely. This time she pushed a loop of the fuse into the charge and tied it off. She continued setting charges until she had a chain that would bring down the trestle as she wanted. At the last, she let the slower main fuse dangle after she had embedded and tied it off and made her way down to its end that was around five feet above the ground.

"Fire in the hole!" she shouted and stuck the igniter.

The fuse burnt at twelve feet a minute. She had less than a minute to get clear and behind the blast wall. She sprinted and tumbled behind the wall with just enough time to grin at Bomber before the first charge blew and the rest went off at about five-second intervals. She poked her head around the end of the blast wall after the last one. The trestle was a pile of wood on the ground.

The rest of the day she had languages and cryptography. She knew French before she arrived and quite a bit of Hindi, but they, the powers that be, wanted her to learn German and Russian as well. As for cryptography, she was familiar with the methods her father used but was now presented with the latest, more sophisticated forms with which she frankly struggled. Encryption was no problem but breaking codes was much harder and involved logical thinking and a penchant for solving puzzles. Above all, it required patience and Beth was not a natural scholar, being more of a practical learner, but she persevered and actually became reasonably good at it.

At the end of most days, she went for a run through the grounds to relax, making use of the terrain and the obstacle course to practise Qinggong. Today, she ran in loose trousers and a blouse that was soon soaked in sweat and transparent despite the cool air. She stopped for a breather at the lake. The view was stunning, the trees just beginning to turn at the onset of autumn.

There was a slight noise behind her. She stayed relaxed but ready. It could be an animal or an assailant.

"I seen you runnin'," a voice she didn't recognise said.

She turned around slowly. A large young man stood two yards away. She assessed him automatically. Five foot ten, about eleven stone, muscular, calloused hands.

"Did you?" she said calmly.

"You be like a deer. Fast and graceful like."

"What are you doing on the estate?" she asked even though she could see he was carrying snares.

"Keepin' the rabbit numbers down. Though they never asked me to."

His eyes dropped to her chest. She was wearing a short corset to support and restrain her breasts under her blouse and the undergarment could be clearly seen through the sweaty material.

When he looked up there was something in his eyes that warned her before he lunged. Instinctively she turned into a hip throw that used his momentum against him forgetting, momentarily, that she was stood on the edge of the bank surrounding the lake. Her assailant gave a cry as he flew through the air to land in the water.

She grinned as she saw him explode to the surface, thrashing his arms and legs. Then the grin turned to a frown. He couldn't swim and the lake was around ten feet deep there.

He went under for a second time. Only his hand showed above the surface.

"Oh bugger," she said as she kicked off her shoes, took a step and arced out in a graceful dive into the water. She dove under and grabbed the boy by the shirt collar. A few kicks saw her at the surface where she dragged him to the shore and pulled him up on the bank. She got him face down and pressed on his back to force any water out of his lungs. He coughed so she left him to recover while she climbed back up to the top.

"And what are you doing, Chaton?" Bomber said.

"Fishing for poachers," she said and slumped to the ground, her back against a tree.

"If I understand all this correctly, the young man, who admits to poaching on the estate grounds, made to take hold of you against your will. You performed a hip throw, and he ended up in the water," the Honourable Rupert Conway, known as Kingfisher, the principle of the academy said.

"That's about it," Beth replied. She had changed into dry clothes, but her hair was still damp.

"And what were you doing at the lake?"

"Running, I often run at the end of the day to relax."

"Hmm, well the young man has been arrested for poaching and will probably go up before the assises in a day or so."

"Won't he tell them about me?" Beth was worried he would be disappeared.

Kingfisher smiled as he stood to look out the window, "Who would believe him? He is five foot ten and a farm labourer who is eleven stones of muscle. You are, what, five feet six and seven stone? Who would believe you could throw him in the lake?"

He had a point.

"In any case it is irrelevant as it is time for you to go out into the field for the next stage of your training. You are ahead of your peers because of what your father and his men have taught you, so you are the first of the current class to be given the opportunity. Do not let us or your father down."

"When do I leave?"

"Patience, my dear, first we have to establish your new identity. Report to Linette to get started first thing tomorrow." Beth left his office and exulted. *Field work! I might even get a mission and Louise is back.*

Linette, aka Louise Thompson, was to all intents, family. She was a former spy and now worked with Beth's mother

Viscountess Caroline Stockley in her business dealings. Linette had worked with her father since he was first inducted into the espionage game. Beth had laughed when she found out his codename was simply M but then found out that only the top agents had monosyllabic codenames. She had made a mental note to ask him about that.

"Do you know where I'm going?" Beth asked Linette as they sat together.

"You will be staying in England," Linette said cryptically.

"It's a big country."

Linette ignored that and opened a packet of papers.

"Your name is Bethany Stockley."

"What?"

"Your name is—"

"I heard. Why am I going out under my own name?"

"Because your subjects will want to use you to get information about your father and his movements."

"This sounds like a mission."

"It is, and also part of your training."

"Who will be my controller?"

"Your father, or in his absence, me."

"Alright, I can live with that." Beth smiled to show she meant that.

"Live with it or not, it is the way it is."

Beth raised one eyebrow at Linette causing her to laugh.

"Let's get on with your briefing. You will go home for Christmas. Your father has a ticket for a party which you will attend on your own. At that party are a group of young members of the Whig party. Your specific target is Mr Gabriel Gershman, he is single, and at the liberal end of the Whigs. He is an idealist, anti-war, against Britain using force to preserve its empire, thinks there should be support for the poor from the central government."

Linette handed over a watercolour picture of a young man with wavy hair and sideburns. He had a weak chin and a long nose.

"Looks like a horse."

"That's as maybe but he is the most attractive man you have ever seen for this mission."

Beth widened her eyes to show she was more than mildly amused by the idea.

"Get to know him at the party, but don't throw yourself at him. Let him know that you might be interested and let him do the chasing. Here is a list of his interests."

Beth read it, basically he was religious, spent time doing good works with the poor, much to his father's annoyance, and liked to ride.

"What about his father?"

"Ahh, now there is a contrast. Gershman senior is a Whig of the old school. A merchant by profession and a landowner. He holds the seat of a rotten borough."

"He looks pretty harmless," Beth said slightly confused as to why he was her subject.

"He would be, except his father is about to retire from politics which will give him the seat," Linette said.

"And he is a pacifist who will push a pacifist agenda."

"Worse, the group he is mixed up with are suspected of operating under the influence of a foreign power who wants to weaken the British hold over the high seas."

"That would hurt everyone."

"Yes, it would. This group already votes against every motion to use the navy to protect the empire and they are getting more members thinking their way every month."

"Idiots, don't they know our prosperity depends on trade by sea."

"Oh, they do but they don't want us to use force to protect it."

The Party

Marty gave Beth all the usual advice when he gave her the ticket but then quite unexpectedly, at Uncle Georgie's Christmas ball, she met Sebastian. She hadn't seen him since Waterloo five years before and hadn't expected to see him again. Yet there he was, tall, strong, tanned, handsome in the uniform of the Rifles. Her heart stopped then restarted with a thundering beat.

Damn, damn, damn, damn, damn, why did he have to show up now? She knew he was linked to the Intelligence Service but also knew she couldn't tell him of her mission. Nevertheless, she spent the whole evening dancing with just him and was sure now he felt about her, the way she felt about him.

This is not going to make my mission any easier, she thought as they parted. Knowing he was at Horse guards or St James's Palace and might get entirely the wrong message if he heard she was associating with Gabriel and his cronies. But then her independent, stubborn side took over and she shut away her feelings for another day.

Beth prepared carefully. The silver-bladed dagger that Georgie had given her for Christmas was on her right thigh, secured by a silk garter. A forty-calibre muff pistol was holstered on her left, she had another in her purse. She wore silk stockings held up above the knee by another pair of garters. She didn't wear a corset as that was too confining, anyway they were going out of fashion, but she did wear a bustier. It was much shorter and had bust cups which allowed her to move from the waist. Over that she wore a deep green dress made of satin trimmed with Dorset lace.

She had selected her jewellery with care, she wanted to show wealth without being flashy or ostentatious. She wore the hair piece that Uncle Georgie had given her that contained hidden lock picks and darts. She carefully coated the darts with a poison that would induce unconsciousness within seconds of it being administered. The tips were, thankfully, sheathed within the gold net of the hairpiece. Around her neck she wore a necklace with a single grape-sized emerald that complemented her dress. On her wrist an emerald bracelet.

As her arms were bare, apart from long silk gloves, she could not wear the forearm sheathed stilettos her father favoured, but she felt she was well enough armed for any contingency. She checked the clock; it was time to go.

The family carriage delivered her to the address, which was a new, fashionable house in the upcoming Paddington area. A servant met her at the door and took her invitation before ushering her inside. The hall was busy with small groups standing around talking. She made her way through them into a room where a buffet had been laid. A servant offered her a tray of drinks and she took a glass of champagne before perusing the food on offer.

"The caviar is divine, it's genuine Beluga from Russia," a woman standing beside her said. She had the hint of an accent.

"I'll try it," Beth said and deposited a small spoonful of the black jewels onto a sliver of melba toast before popping into her mouth. The salty, fishy eggs of the sturgeon exploded across her tongue. "It's wonderful."

"Catarina Vallance… and you are?"

"Bethany Stockley."

"You know the Gershmans?"

"Not personally. I was invited by Eldridge Porter." That was a sustainable lie as he was out of the country at the moment. "It's a shame he isn't here as I really don't know anybody else."

Catarina looked her over appraisingly. Beth resisted the urge to go into a twirl so she could be examined from all sides.

"Come, let me introduce you to Gabriel and some of his friends."

"Oh! That would be just lovely," Beth gushed.

Gabriel was in a group of five. Three men and two women.

"Gabriel, darling. Look who I found; this is Bethany Stockley."

Gabriel turned and looked at her, his eyes widening as he took in the site of a beautiful woman. "Why, Catarina, I do believe you have competition for the most beautiful woman at the party."

Catarina leaned in and said something quietly to him. He looked chagrined for a moment then recovered. Beth noted it while appearing to wait patiently.

"Is your father Viscount Stockley?" Gabriel said.

"Yes, Daddy is in London before going on to Dorset with Mummy. He is going away again in the new year."

"Is he really?" Gabriel said thoughtfully. "I haven't heard that the government is sending the navy anywhere."

"He will be back for the coronation. Uncle Georgie would be furious if he missed that," Beth said with wide-eyed innocence.

"Uncle Georgie?"

"Ooh sorry, I meant the king. He is my godfather you know."

One of the women smirked. "He will not be on the throne for long."

"Emily," her partner warned sharply. Emily shut her mouth, but the smirk stayed.

"His health isn't good. I do worry about him," Beth said sadly.

"We can all pray he lives for a long and prosperous reign," her partner continued. He nodded a bow, "Charles Tallamy, at your service. This is my wife, Emily."

"Charmed," Beth said with the hint of a curtsy.

"While we are making introductions," the oldest of the group, a man of around fifty years with a French accent, said, "Charles Fourier and my companion Sylvie."

Beth knew of Fourier. He was a radical out of the French revolution and espoused Utopian Socialism. She had read his book in preparation.

"Monsieur Fourier, I am so pleased to meet you I have read, *Théorie des quatre mouvements et des destinées générales.*"

"You have? I thought that was only available in Paris."

"I found a copy in a market in Paris. It was very interesting. I find the concept of socialism intriguing."

"You have been deceiving us, my dear," Catrina said. Beth looked at her inquiringly. "You are not as vapid as you would have us believe."

"I behave as society expects." Beth looked her directly in the eye. "I find coming over as too intelligent makes a lot of people feel challenged."

"You have no need to hide your intellect here, my dear," Gabriel said, "we value it equally from men and women."

The discussion continued and Beth was drawn into the group. She argued for or against different theories put up by Tallamy and Fourier along with the others. Eventually Gabriel asked her if she would dance.

About time!

They danced a waltz, then he swung her into the latest Viennese version which could have made her dizzy if she hadn't known how to spot.

"You are a dancer?" Gabriel asked at the end of the dance.

"Why do you ask?"

"Most women don't know how to avoid getting dizzy."

"I practise ballet."

"What else do you – practise?"

"You wouldn't believe me if I told you," Beth replied with more than a hint of intrigue.

"Your father and mother are both renowned for their skills with a blade. Do you fence?"

"A little, it never really appealed to me. I prefer to ride."

Hook baited.

"I love to ride as well. Would you join me at the park?" he said, meaning Hyde Park.

"I would have to ask Daddy. He is quite strict on things like that."

Beth noticed that Catarina watched her and Gabriel all the time. She would have to look into her at some point but now was definitely not the time. She let Gabriel steer her back to the group where she discussed the philosophy of Rousseau and Voltaire.

All that boring reading is paying off. As they got onto the subject of female emancipation.

"Should all women have the vote? Wouldn't most just vote the way their husbands tell them?" Tallamy said.

"Phht as if I would," his wife slurred; she was getting progressively drunk.

"I think we should be going," Tallamy said as his wife downed another glass of champagne. He put her arm through his and practically frogmarched her to the door.

"Poor Charles, Emily always has a problem dealing with her drink," Gabriel said.

Beth had no such problem. She had been pouring at least half of everything she was given into an aspidistra.

"Daddy is in the navy, we were taught to drink at an early age," she said.

"What do you think about what he does?"

"I really don't know what he does. He disappears off for months or even years at a time."

"Don't you want to see more of him?"

This was her opening.

"Oh yes! I'd love to. Being at war like we were with Napoleon was one thing but running around bullying people like the Indians is too much!"

"Have you been to India?"

"Yes, and the Company just treats the poor Indians like slaves."

"That is our point! We are against the use of force in any form to coerce people into trading with us."

Beth felt she should put up a token resistance.

"But what about when a country is dominating markets and shutting us out? Like the Dutch in the East Indies."

"Talk of that is just an excuse to send in the gunships. They were there first so they are entitled to some sort of monopoly. We must be prepared to compete on financial terms, and they must be prepared to trade fairly."

That is a very ideal world. I've never met a Dutchman yet who would give up an advantage, Beth thought but managed to look half convinced and continued to argue.

"What if they rebel, what are we to do then?"

"If the natives of a country don't want us there, we shouldn't be there."

"Well, that's just naïve, we would have no empire at all if we all thought like that."

"Why do we need an empire? Britain would be better without one."

"How?"

"If we were to follow socialist ideology, we would all work for the common good. No kings or queens or emperors. All men would be equal. What we need to do is persuade the world to follow it and it will end all wars."

Beth had to exert extreme control. This man was dangerous. That ideology would turn the world on its head and there was no way the powers that be would allow that.

"That sounds very like what the revolutionaries in France were saying before the terror," Beth said.

"It is. They took a wrong turn. There was no need to massacre the wealthy or the intelligentsia. The redistribution of wealth can be done via taxation and the country run by the higher educated."

"You mean academics?"

"Yes, they would run the country on purely scientific principles."

Beth wanted to ask a whole lot more questions, but she had heard enough already to decide that Gabriel was a well-meaning, if deluded man. What she needed to know was whether he was being spurred on by someone else.

Her eye fell on Catarina who was looking at the two of them. She smiled as she thought, *I am going to find out just who you are.*

The Contessa

Beth took her favourite mare, Melody, an Arab cross Welsh Cob, out for a hack around Hyde Park. She rode side saddle, even though she preferred to ride astride, but to do so would be scandalous. Side saddle wasn't so bad, and an expert practitioner could do almost everything a man could do. She was dressed fashionably in a riding habit and wore a French-style top hat with a black lace veil.

She was escorted by one of the house footmen who rode a grey gelding named Sabre. Sabre was a former cavalry mount from the Lifeguards. The footman, William Crow, had been in the 3rd Regiment of the King's Own Light Dragoons and was an expert horseman and fighter.

She entered the park via Grosvenor Gate and turned left to head down towards Hyde Park Corner. She held Melody to a walk until she had a clear road ahead then she nudged her into a trot. She would have loved to go into a canter and Melody was eager to run but the park was no place for it as there were too many pedestrians.

"Hello, Miss Bethany," a familiar voice called.

She slowed Melody to a walk and then to a stop. Gabriel, riding a tall blood, approached.

"Hello, Gabriel," she replied. "That's a fine-looking horse."

"This is Horatio, I named him after Nelson. He is unbeatable. Can I accompany you?"

"Certainly."

They walked for a while and chatted about the weather and the park. Then Beth said, "Does Miss Vallance not ride?"

"She does. Why do you ask?"

"Why, I thought you were a couple."

Gabriel laughed heartily. "Oh no, I am not her beau. She is fiercely independent."

They approached the Horse Guards' barracks that lay on the southern edge of the park.

"Does she reside in London? I have never seen her at any of the balls. A beauty such as her would be hard to miss."

"Competition?" Gabriel teased.

"I am just a girl. I cannot compete with her."

Gabriel looked at her earnestly. "You are as much a beauty as she is."

Beth blushed at the compliment.

"It's strange that I have never seen her," she said to cover her embarrassment.

"She doesn't circulate much apart from with the group."

Now, that is strange, any woman with her looks would be invited to most parties and balls.

"She is holding a soirée this evening at her house in Portland Street. Would you like to come?"

"I would be delighted. Shall we canter down the King's Road?"

"Beth, that is his private road."

Beth laughed then grinned mischievously.

"I'm sure Uncle Georgie won't mind. Come on!"

She cut across the grass to the road which was a short way to the north. It was empty of any traffic as people confined themselves to the footpath that ran beside it.

Gabriel followed with William close behind. As soon as she hit the road, she let Melody have her head. The spirited mare leapt forward in a gallop. Gabriel caught her up quickly on his big blood.

"I thought you said a canter?" he shouted across to her over the thunder of hooves.

Beth didn't reply, she was having too much fun.

"OY, YOU. STOP."

It was a policeman who had stepped out into the road ahead of them. Beth pulled Melody up in front of the officer.

Her horse's haunches almost on the ground as she pulled her up.

"Hello, Constable Quigley," she said brightly.

"Oh, it's you, Miss Bethany, now you know you shouldn't be on the king's private road."

"I'm sure he won't mind. He is my godfather you know."

"That's as maybe, Miss, but if I let you ride on here then everyone will . Who is that with you?"

"Constable Quigley, may I present Mr Gabriel Gershman."

"Sir, I am sure you know the rules of the park. You should not let Miss Bethany lead you astray," Constable Quigley admonished. "Now the pair of you walk your horses to the end and re-join the public path."

As he rode past the constable, William rolled his eyes as if to say, *what can I do?* The constable raised his eyebrows in secret agreement. "Young people have no common sense," he said, sotto voice.

Gabriel had given Beth the address in Portland Street. It was a nice house of the Palladian school of architecture. Fairly new and owned by the Gershmans. Beth had done her homework. She had also made enquiries about Catarina Vallance through James Turner. She fully expected to find she didn't exist.

In the meantime, she would use this opportunity to case the house for a visit one night. It was only a short carriage ride to the address and the coach pulled up directly outside the door of the house that was located in a terrace. Beth alighted, a teenage boy walking along the pavement gawped at her. She had chosen her outfit carefully. First and most important it concealed her weapons and several tools. Second and almost equally important it was verging on scandalously sexy without making her look like a tart. She was going to get and hold Gabriel's attention.

Her father had opened his mouth to say something then snapped it shut when he saw her leave the house. Something in his eyes told her he wasn't seeing her as his little girl anymore. The look had been proud but slightly sad. He had kissed her on the cheek and told her to be bold.

She was let in by a servant and shown into the drawing room where the same group of people she had met at the party were having a lively discussion about the merits of the latest laws being passed in parliament.

Gabriel looked up as she entered, and his jaw hit his chest. Catarina saw and turned to her. There was the hint of a frown before she plastered on a welcoming smile. *Got you*, Beth inwardly cheered.

"Bethany! Welcome to my home," Catarina said.

"Thank you. I am pleased to be here."

Gabriel stood and bowed over her hand.

"You look ravishing," he said quietly, then louder, "you must join in the conversation. We are discussing the extension of the Alien Act."

Beth knew the Alien Act was in place to allow the government to remove undesirable foreigners from the United Kingdom and that Lord Castlereagh was trying to get a bill passed to extend it. She could have expounded on it but played the naïve, closeted daughter of a rich man instead.

"What does that do?"

"It allows the government to expel people from the kingdom that they don't like."

"What? Anybody?" she gasped.

"Well, not citizens but foreigners," Gabriel said.

"That's just mean!"

"I'm glad you see it the same way I do."

"How many have been treated this way?"

"Too many and most without adequate cause."

Beth knew that was a blatant exaggeration or even a lie as there were currently twenty-five thousand foreign people living in England. A large increase on the number in 1818 admittedly. Many were in the kingdom for trade and were covered by older statutes such as the Magna Charta but there was an increasing proportion who weren't. In any case in the last two years only a handful had been expelled mainly because they were foreign agents. With Europe in constant flux, there were secret and not so secret trade wars, and the government saw it as a necessity to control the number coming in and to give them the ability to evict those that posed a threat.

"My goodness, those poor people. How can we stop this?" Beth gasped.

"That is what we are discussing."

The discussion continued with Charles Fourier putting forward an elegant argument for the freedom of movement. Beth sat wide eyed listening to every word which she would include in her report.

"What do you think, Catarina?" Beth said as if looking to the older woman for guidance.

"I agree that such an act is cruel and unnecessary. It does nothing but damage trade and the movement of individuals throughout the world."

Beth enthusiastically joined in the discussion which turned more and more into a plan of action to delay and even defeat the bill that Lord Castlereagh was trying to get through.

Eventually the quantity of tea took its inevitable toll and Beth had to ask where she could 'powder her nose'.

"You can use the commode in my bedroom," Catarina told her. The house toilet was a thunder box in the back garden, and it was chilly out there.

Beth went up the stairs to the bedroom and made use of the commode. She checked the window, noting the latch, and when she left the room checked the hallway floor for squeaks. A window overlooked the back garden that she could see backed onto the terraced houses in the street behind this one.

The next day she carried out a reconnaissance of the street and found a passage at the end of the terrace that led to the rear gardens. She walked along it. Halfway down it crossed a path that went between the back-to-back gardens. She followed the path to Catarina's house. There was a gate which was securely locked on the inside.

Back at the family home she found a letter waiting for her. It was encrypted. She locked herself in her father's study and decoded it.

Catarina Vallance: Not registered on the census or with any governmental or local departments. We suspect she is Polish Lithuanian, Contessa Catarina Lesniak. Her father is a military commander in the Imperial Russian army. She is suspected of being a member of their Intelligence Service and is considered to be dangerous. If it is her, act with extreme caution.

"Now that is interesting and would explain why she wants freedom of movement," Beth said to herself. She took a sheet of paper and wrote a note, folded it then rang the bell. When a servant appeared she said, "Have this delivered to Major Ashley-Cooper." She sat and thought her ideas through, discarding some and putting the other together into the beginnings of a plan.

Sebastian visited that evening. He was intrigued, the message simply said, *I need your help. B.* Beth was waiting for him in her father's study and stepped into his arms as soon as the door was closed. They kissed, long and lingering then Beth pulled away.

"I'm on a mission and need your help."

"I'm all yours."

Beth took that both ways.

"I need to break into the house of someone we think is a Russian agent trying to influence a faction of the Whigs."

"Interesting. Why?"

"To establish her identity and why she is here."

"Why me?"

"Because I can trust you."

Sebastian grinned. "With your life."

"I know, the target is extremely dangerous." She grinned back knowing he meant more.

"When?"

"Are you off duty tomorrow evening?"

"My watch finishes at nine."

"Perfect. Can you meet me here at eleven?"

"If we can have dinner tonight."

"Of course."

There was a knock at the door.

"Yes?" Beth called.

"Dinner is served, Miss."

"Looks like it's ready."

Sebastian arrived at the house, dressed in a dark suit with a dark overcoat and hat. He was armed. A servant showed him into Martin's study. Beth was preparing and taking items from her father's equipment cupboard.

"This is the stuff he leaves at home?" Sebastian said as he scanned the contents. There was everything needed to break into a house from lockpicks to slim jims and a variety of knives, coshes, and pistols. He picked up and weighed a set of knuckle dusters.

"He likes to have everything to hand, so there are similar cupboards in all our houses."

"Sounds like the Martin I know and love."

"Do you need anything?"

"A cosh would be useful. What's in the tin flask?"

"Ether."

"Does she have servants?"

"Hmm, yes."

Sebastian picked up the flask and a wad of cloth and stuffed both in his pocket.

Beth wore a black one-piece coverall. It fitted in all the right places as far as Sebastian was concerned. She pulled a cloak around her shoulders which covered her from neck to toe.

"Time to go."

An unmarked carriage carried them to the end of the road where Catarina lived. Beth knew she wasn't at the house as she was attending a meeting of the emergent socialist party in Coventry in the west midlands. She left the cloak on the seat and led Sebastian through the passage to the back of the house. He cupped his hands and boosted her over the gate then jumped up and pulled himself over.

They waited in the dark to see if there was any movement inside. Satisfied that everyone was asleep they went to the scullery door which was down several steps. Beth quickly picked the lock, and they slipped inside. It was as dark as pitch, so Sebastian lit a small, shuttered lantern. The door to the kitchen was open and Beth slipped through. She stopped suddenly and held out her hand. There on the floor, fast asleep, was a scullery maid.

They stepped quietly around her and made their way to the door into the house. They froze as the girl muttered in her sleep and turned over on the thin mattress. When she had settled, they opened the door and slipped into the house proper.

"Hopefully the rest of the servants will be up in the garret." Sebastian whispered. They climbed the stairs to the ground floor. A quick search revealed that one door was locked. Beth unlocked it. Inside they found a study and after they closed the curtains Beth lit the gaslights.

"You search, I will keep watch." Sebastian slipped out into the hallway

Beth started with the desk, she worked her way methodically through the drawers from bottom to top, relocking them after she had finished. Finding nothing of real interest she made sure everything was as she had found it and moved on to search the rest of the room.

"Nothing there. Not even a safe," she whispered and moved to the stairs to the first floor.

"Did you open the curtains?" Sebastian checked with her.

"Yes," Beth replied, moving like a shadow.

"Her bedroom," Beth stopped in surprise, "it's locked."

Sebastian waited while Beth examined the door carefully. She found a fine thread stuck across from the door to the jam. *Someone is being very careful.* She carefully lifted it from the jam, stuck it to the door with some saliva and picked the lock. The door opened soundlessly.

Leaving it open she used the shuttered lantern to cross the room and close the drapes. She pulled Sebastian inside and closed the door.

"Light that lamp." She indicated an oil lamp on a side table.

They searched the walls, looking behind every picture.

Nothing.

They opened every wardrobe and drawer.

Nothing.

They searched the floor minutely. Nothing.

Beth stood and looked around the room.

"The commode."

Sebastian's eyebrows raised and he looked at the object sceptically.

Beth opened the top. The pot was inside and clean thankfully. She lifted it out, put it to one side and turned her attention to the sides of the box like the cavity it had sat in. She knocked the sides which all sounded solid enough. She tapped the bottom. *Did that sound different?* She compared the sound of the bottom and the sides. There was definitely a difference.

She took a slim jim and gently pushed it into the gap between the base and the side. It stopped on the forward edge. She tried it from the opposite corner. It stopped a half inch short of the last probe.

There must be a catch and a catch must have a release.

She felt around the cavity then moved her attention to the front of the commode. There were raised carvings decorating it and Beth focussed on those. One moved, ever so slightly.

She pressed. Nothing.

She checked the rest of the carving. Another moved slightly.

She pressed the two together. Nothing.

She tried twisting them. The one on the left turned clockwise, the one on the right anticlockwise. But still nothing happened.

She pressed again. They moved and there was a click. The floor of the cavity sprung up.

"Ta da!" she whispered.

Inside were papers. Some in English, some obviously encrypted and others in Russian. Thanking the academy for teaching her Russian she quickly read the documents in Cyrillic. It identified the holder as Contessa Catarina Lesniak. There was an address in St Petersburg which she noted. The rest were letters from her father and mother. The encrypted letters would have to wait. She put everything back as it had been, carefully closed the lid and put the pot back in before putting the catches back to their original position.

"Let's go."

They cracked open the door and listened before exiting into the hall. The door was relocked, and the thread put back into place. They slipped silently downstairs to the kitchen. Just as she was about to open the door, they heard a sound. Beth listened and she noticed light leaking from under the door.

"What is it?" Sebastian whispered.

"I think the maid is preparing dough to make bread," Beth whispered back. We will have to go out the front door."

They slipped back upstairs and to the hallway. The door was bolted on the inside. They couldn't leave that way without someone noticing.

"Damn," Beth swore. She remembered there was a bay window at the back of the house on that floor. "Come on."

The bay looked over the garden and had a sash window in the centre. Sebastian slipped the catch and gently put pressure on it to move it up. It was stuck. He applied more pressure, and it gave with a squeak.

They froze and listened. There was no sign that anybody had noticed. He opened it fully and Beth climbed out, dropping lightly to the ground. Sebastian followed using a slim jim to reset the catch after he closed the window.

Kidnap

Beth sat outside James Turner's office which was in the Foreign Office building. She had been told to report to him rather than the boss of the Domestic Intelligence Branch. He was apparently on his way back from a meeting with George Canning. She sat with a cup of tea and waited. His secretary, a stern older woman with half-moon glasses for reading sat at her desk copying a document.

Beth was about to try and talk to her when the door opened, and James Turner arrived.

"Hello, Chaton, sorry to keep you waiting," he said and ushered her into his inner sanctum. She was vaguely disappointed that it was a plain, utilitarian room. With just a pair of club chairs for comfort.

"You have your report?"

Beth nodded and handed it over. Turner sat back and read it.

"We were right then, she is Contessa Catarina Lesniak," Turner said out loud. Beth assumed it was rhetorical.

"Charles Fourier? Huh, I might have known he would be in there somewhere."

He finished reading.

"Do you think Gabriel knows who Catarina really is?"

"No, I don't think any of the British in that group do."

"What do you think she is after?"

"To damage our ability to defend our trade. The whole Aliens bill thing is an aside."

The door opened and George Canning came in.

"Chaton," he greeted her, then looked at Turner. "Well?"

"It's who we thought it is and she is trying to subvert parliament into voting away our sea defences."

"Who else knows about your investigation?"

"Major Ashley-Cooper. He helped me break into her house."

"Lancelot? I should have guessed you would be his Guinevere. Maybe we should change your code name."

Beth blushed and he relented. "Just joking. I saw you two dancing at the easter ball."

Turner drew Canning's attention back to the problem in hand, "Charles Fourier is spreading his seditious nonsense to them as well."

"Is he?" Canning suddenly brightened. "I think we can turn this to our advantage."

"How so?" Turner said.

"By presenting parliament with a confidential briefing before deporting the two of them."

"I will have her house watched around the clock and set a team to watch Fourier."

"Will you be visiting them again?" Canning asked Beth.

"They have a meeting every Friday at either her house or Gabriel's."

"Good, attend the next one. We don't want to tip our hand too soon, but we also don't want her getting away with any information. I want you to steal her papers."

Beth went riding with Gabriel again, only this time stuck to the park rules and kept Melody to a trot.

"Something strange happened at the House yesterday," Gabriel said. Beth interpreted that as the House of Commons.

"Oh, what was that?"

"There were rumours of a secret briefing, then when I asked our whips about it, they denied all knowledge."

"What's strange about that? It was a rumour and could have been false."

"I suppose it could have been that. Father also said he had heard it, but no one seemed to have any firm facts. It's damn unusual whatever the case, as rumours of briefings almost always turn out to be true."

Beth changed the subject to some innocent observations of other park users.

"What does your father think of being sent off to bully our colonies and competitors?" Gabriel suddenly asked, interrupting her.

"He says he doesn't get involved in politics. He is a sailor and does what the government and king ask him to."

"That is just acting as the government's hammer."

"Actually, he is more than that," Beth replied, annoyed. "He opposes slavery and wants everyone to have a say in how their country is run."

"But he is still a member of the East India Company, and they are the biggest oppressor of all."

"He was given his shares as a reward for solving the problem of the Madagascar pirates. You cannot tell me he got wounded and men died there for nothing."

"There is an exception to every rule."

Pompous ass.

"Is there a meeting tomorrow?"

"Yes, at Catarina's. She will tell us about the gathering of the Socialist Society in Coventry."

Beth arrived at Catarina's house a little late on Friday. The discussion was in full swing.

"You are all very exercised, what is the matter?"

Gabriel looked at her, the others went quiet.

"There is to be a confidential briefing, Beth. It is to be about the Aliens Act."

"Oh? Do you know what it will say?"

"Yes, I do. It will say that some undesirable foreigners are being deported."

"Who?" Beth asked using all her acting skills to appear calm.

"A Frenchman and his wife and a Russian Contessa."

"A French—" she looked at Fourier and his companion. "They can't deport you!"

"They can and will my dear," Fourier said.

"The question is who is the Russian Contessa?" Gabriel said.

The question is how did you find this out?

Catarina suddenly went to the window and looked out from behind the curtain.

"There are men in the street, a lot of men. Police as well," she said.

"What?" Fourier jumped to his feet. "Your man told us nothing would happen until next week."

Catarina turned around to Beth, a gun in her hand. "You will come with me."

"Catarina?" Gabriel said.

There was banging at the front door followed by shouts, "Police. Open up!"

"She told them we would all be here tonight; she is an agent."

"Why does that matter to you?"

"Because she is the Russian Contessa," Beth said.

"What? Russian?" Gabriel said.

The banging on the door turned into the sound of cracking. Catarina moved fast and was suddenly behind Beth with the gun at her head.

The door burst open and there stood Admiral Turner flanked by two armed policemen.

"Stay where you are," Catarina commanded.

The tableau froze. Gabriel and the other English, open mouthed in shock. Fourier sneered disdainfully. Turner and the police stood with guns in hand.

Turner took command, "Let's not be hasty. Put down the gun."

Catarina looked at him defiantly. "So you can take me in and interrogate me? I don't think so. If you want her back alive you will let me and the Fouriers pass.

"You have nowhere to go."

"We will leave the country on our terms."

"No matter, we will still tell the same story to the commons."

"I am sure you will but you will not have us to parade as proof."

"Catarina—" Gabriel said.

"Shut up, you fool. This is your fault."

While that was going on Beth exchanged an entire conversation with Turner using hand signals. Turner put his gun away, "Very well, you can go but if any harm comes to Bethany, I will hunt you down and kill you."

"She will be released as soon as we are safely on French soil."

Catarina didn't collect any clothes, just had Beth pick up a leather bag from the hallway. Then, holding Beth close, she manoeuvred them all out of the house to the Fourier's carriage and ordered the driver to go. Once they were away from the house, she told him to head to the river and St Catherine's dock.

They had gagged and bound Beth but she could still hear what they said. As she had never used a foreign language in front of them, they spoke in French thinking she wouldn't understand.

"What will we do with her once we get to France?" Fourier said.

"We could kill her but that would bring the wrath of her father down on us and he is not one to hold back. No, we will release her as I said."

"How will we get to France?" Sylvie, Fourier's mistress or wife, whatever she was, asked in a frightened voice.

"I have a ship at St Catherine's dock, it is ready to sail at a moment's notice."

"What will you do afterwards?"

"I will go back to St Petersburg."

So, Fourier knew she was a Russian agent.

Beth was working on the bindings that held her wrists behind her back. They had been well tied but she had been trained how to hold her arms just so to keep bindings from being too tight. Now she was working a loop down over the ball of her thumb.

The coach turned and there was an echo as it passed through a passageway or covered gate. *That's strange, I don't remember there being a covered entrance to St. Catherine's Dock.*

The coach stopped. Fourier got out followed by Sylvie then Catarina pushed Beth out. They were in the courtyard of a house.

"This way," Catarina said, and led them into the house. The coachman followed.

Inside she collected together papers and a travel trunk.

"What is this place?" Sylvie asked.

"A safe house. I keep my most important things here. It backs onto the dock. Come. You bring the trunk."

"Yes, Ma'am," the coachman said.

Beth looked at him sharply as she thought she recognised his voice. He looked across at her as he picked up the trunk and winked.

What? Who is that?

Catarina pushed her ahead of her before she could get a good look at the man. They went down into the cellar. Catarina opened a door with a key on her chatelaine and they entered a passage. It was damp and water dripped from the ceiling leaving little calcified stalagmites hanging down.

At the end, there were steps going up to a trapdoor. They were slippery with slime and Beth had to be held up as she slipped on the first one. She used the distraction to get the loop over her thumb. The rope was now loose enough to slip off, but she waited.

They emerged into a warehouse that was stacked with crates. Beth noted the markings were Russian. Catarina led them to a spot near the doors and bade them sit while she went outside. Fourier loosened Beth's gag and pulled it down below her chin.

"I'm not a spy, I didn't tell anyone about anything," she sobbed.

Fourier looked at her sympathetically, "I don't think you are, but Catarina has been jealous of you from the start."

"Jealous of me? Why?"

"Because of your youth and looks and the effect you had on Gabriel."

The door opened and Catarina entered with a man who looked like a sailor.

"This is Captain Slivanovic, he will take you to France."

"You are not joining us?" Fourier said.

"No, I am going home."

"And the girl?"

"She is going with me."

The door opened again and a tall elegantly dressed man in a top hat came in. Beth kept her head down.

"Catarina, I don't think that is a good idea," he said in Russian.

Catarina looked defiantly at him, "Ambassador, this is a matter for the secret service."

"Not when it involves the kidnapping of the daughter of a British peer."

"He is a spy and so is she."

"You have no proof of that."

"We will get the truth out of her."

The ambassador sighed. "You have become a liability, my dear." He nodded to the coachman who pulled a gun from his coat pocket.

"What are you doing?"

"Your political leanings are not in line with the interests of the tsar. You have been removed from the service."

"But—" she started to say when there was a shot.

She looked down at her chest, a look of surprise on her face. A red rose bloomed above her heart. As she slid to the ground the door opened and Admiral Turner walked in.

"Job done, thank you, Ambassador." He stepped over to Beth.

"Are you unharmed, my dear?" he said with a warning look.

"Yes, thank you, Uncle James."

Turner turned to the Fouriers. "You will be deported most publicly."

Beth looked around; the coachman had disappeared. Turner smiled at her, then at the Fouriers.

"Beth wasn't the agent, the coachman was."

The Fouriers were deported, and it was all over the front pages of the news across Britain. The stories told of seditious behaviour, that they were trying to subvert the law of the land and parliament and corrupting the innocents. The Alien Act bill was passed with a comfortable majority.

Beth reported to Turner's office.

"No one outside of the service associates you with the operation," James said once Beth was seated. "They have been told that the coachman was the spy, which was true to an extent as he does indeed work for us."

"Who was it? I thought I recognised him but his disguise was too good, and he winked at me."

"A fellow classmate of yours, Brindle."

"Brindle? I didn't recognise him."

"He has shown an aptitude for disguise and ruthlessness. He will go far."

Beth shook her head in wonder. She wouldn't have put Brindle down as one to shoot someone, let alone a woman, in cold blood.

"Life is full of surprises. What happened to Catarina's body?"

"The Russian Embassy took it and is shipping it to her family. The official story is that she was killed on a mission, which is true."

"A half-truth being more believable than an outright lie." Beth sighed.

"I do have some personal news for you. You have graduated from the academy."

"I have?"

"Yes, and furthermore you are on my staff."

"What? I mean, that is wonderful, but I thought I was destined for Internal?"

"Your performance and demonstrated ability with languages persuaded George to put you here. Especially as we have another mission for you. You will be teamed with a senior agent as you are still only a journeyman."

Surrey

Beth and her new partner attended a briefing with Admiral Turner and George Canning. Her partner was Alain Fitznorton, codename Archer, who hailed from the Welsh Marches and could claim the Marcher Lord Norton as an ancestor. The Fitz prefix just meant he was from a branch of the family that was the by-blow of an affair between the king and the lord's daughter Lady Elizabeth Norton.

Archer was an inch or so taller than Beth, broad shouldered, with brown hair and eyes, and reasonably good looking. He spoke several languages including French and Russian and was a specialist in infiltration although he had the same broad range of skills Beth had.

"The two of you are to pose as newlyweds. Archer will be the Right Honourable Charlton Manning. Chaton, you are Sylvia Manning," Canning said and a packet was placed in front of each of them. "These are your papers and backgrounds; learn them and destroy any papers you do not need to carry. The packet also gives you the contact who will introduce you to the court."

Turner took over. "We have been asked by the king to help one of his relatives and we want you to establish what is going on in the court of Tsar Alexander 1st. There are rumours that he is becoming a recluse. We also want to know what the reaction of the court is. Are there factions who want him to be overthrown? Or are there plots to assassinate him?"

"What the mood of the court is, factions, plots. Understood," Beth said.

"Find and cultivate people in the court who are sympathetic to Britain. We also want you to try and find out who was behind Catarina and eliminate one or two to let them know to keep their shenanigans to their own country. You leave next Friday on the regular packet to St Petersburg."

Beth settled into a comfortable chair and opened the packet. In it were identity papers, a visa to enter Russia, a comprehensive biography of her character and that of her spouse. She concentrated on the biography.

Sylvia Grace Manning ne Arbuthnot. Father Sydney Matthew Arbuthnot, Mother Charlotte Grace Arbuthnot, deceased. Mother died of typhus on September 11th, 1818. Sylvia is an only child, born August 5th, 1798.

That makes me twenty-two-years old. I'm a grown up!

Family home is in Herefordshire in the county town, Hereford, where her father was a wool merchant. He is now in bedlam due to the grief of losing her mother.

That probably means there is a man in bedlam with that name.

Sylvia lived at home and was educated by a tutor. She met her future husband at the Herefordshire Hunt. She is an excellent rider both with a normal and side saddle and one of her passions is hunting. Her marriage was brokered by her aunt who had ambitions that the family be linked to the aristocracy. The Mannings are titled (Baron) but poor because of inheritance tax, the Arbuthnots are wealthy, and Sylvia is the sole heir to her father's fortune which is considerable.

Charlton Manning professes to have fallen for Sylvia at first sight.

Bleugh, someone is having a romantic moment.

He is also an excellent rider to hounds and is the only son. He already manages the estate on behalf of his father who is approaching seventy years old. Charlton is thirty. His parents had their only child quite late in life. Despite all that, the couple are happily married.

After their honeymoon the couple will live in a house on the Manning estate in Credenhill. It is the gatehouse to the manor and is a large Tudor building built in the reign of Elizabeth I. Sylvia also has her father's house in trust.

So far so easy, Beth thought and carried on.

What followed was a comprehensive biography, family tree and list of acquaintances which gave rise to the thought that this woman must surely exist. She had a meeting scheduled with Turner and Linette in the morning, and would have to ask. She read on and found out that their contact was Grand Duchess Catherine Pavlovna, sister of the tsar, married to King William I of Württemberg who was at the Russian court for the whole year.

At the 'office' the next day Beth and Archer were quizzed on what they had memorised by a severe woman dressed in black. She insisted they only used their cover names and were in character at all times.

They were shown into Turner's office after the woman had reported to him. Turner sat them down and said, "You both need to spend more time on your characters. I have arranged for you to join the Surrey Hunt at Clandon on Saturday. You have been introduced by the master of hounds of the Huntingdonshire Hunt. That will give you the opportunity to bed your characters in and get to know each other better.

You can take your own horses; I have a horsebox booked. You have been invited to stay with the Earl of Onslow at Clandon Park House. You leave first thing in the morning. We have had new luggage made for you which is being delivered to your London addresses as we speak. The two of you will live as husband and wife from now on and while in London stay at the Red Lion in Westminster. Move there today. Any questions?"

"Yes," Beth said. "Does this couple exist?"

"Astute as always. They did. They were killed on their wedding day when their carriage overturned on the road to Bristol. A tragic accident but one that gave us the opportunity to have you adopt their lives for a while."

"Won't there be a record of their deaths?"

"Not until you finish your mission. As far as their loved ones are concerned, they are still on their grand Tour. We are sending them letters to cover that."

Beth dyed her hair brown covering up her auburn locks and used makeup to alter her skin tone. She packed her things in the luggage that had been provided. It was made by Liberty and carried her monogram SM. Her wardrobe consisted of dresses that were just six months out of date, riding habits, bonnets and hats, a selection of shoes and boots and her undergarments. Her trunks also had a range of hidden compartments where she concealed her weapons, makeup, wigs, disguises and housebreaking tools.

She placed a muff pistol in her purse and another in her muff. Wore her daggers in their garter sheathes and her hat pins were extra-long and made of steel. The footmen loaded her baggage onto an open carriage, asked no questions and wished her a fond farewell. She collected Archer and they settled into the Red Lion.

The moment had come that Beth had worried about as she stood facing the large canopied double bed. Archer paid the men that had carried their luggage up to their room and turned to see her standing there.

"Well, Mrs Manning, shall we dress for dinner?" he said with a poorly concealed grin.

"Um, where, I mean how, will we sleep?"

"I will sleep very well thank you."

"That's not what I meant."

"I know. This is your first mission acting as a married woman. I expect it will take time to get used to it."

"Couldn't we have separate rooms? Some people do."

"On our honeymoon?"

She had to admit he had her there.

"You are shy. It is alright, I will be very discreet."

"I am sure you will."

All the same she went into the small dressing room to change.

The next morning the coach was waiting for them with a two-horse box pulled by a pair of Shires. The Shires were both at least seventeen hands and brushed until their coats shone and the white feathers on his forelegs glowed. The harness brasses gleamed in the sun and the leather shone. Inside the box Melody and Archer's, rather Charlton's, blood gelding were comfortable and warm despite the nip in the air. They had also been groomed and clipped to perfection, their tack oiled and polished.

Beth slept fitfully, not being used to sharing a bed. She had prepared for sleep in private and worn her usual cotton nightdress that covered her from neck to ankle. She knew her parents slept naked when they were together, and her mother only wore a nightdress when her father was away. But she had never slept in such close proximity to a man and had only the thin cotton between her and him. It stirred some interesting emotions.

Archer was a complete gentleman and didn't seem to be bothered that she was almost naked beside him, and that, if she was honest, bothered her as well. *Am I not attractive? Isn't he attracted to me? What would it be like if —"* she stopped that thought before it started.

The trip to Clandon was uneventful, the coach didn't even have to change horses. They pulled up in front of Clandon Park house. Designed by Giacomo Leoni in the Palladian style in the early 18th century. It had three stories, was rectangular in form, with four square columns holding up a lintel above the second-floor windows. The gardens were magnificent,

"Designed by Capability Brown," Lady Georgiana, who greeted them, said when she saw Beth admiring the gardens.

"Daddy is in London. He was called to parliament late yesterday; he sends his apologies and will return as soon as he can".

Georgiana was older than Beth and the youngest child of Thomas Onslow by his second wife who had died the year before. His sons from his first marriage were married. Arthur lived at the house with his wife and Thomas lived at Stoke Park near Guildford.

"You will meet Arthur and Mary at dinner. Mary is horribly pregnant. It's due at any time."

Beth decided Georgina was rather empty headed and a flibbertigibbet who had no idea of their real identities.

"Were you at the king's easter ball?" Beth asked.

"Why no I wasn't. Mamma and Pappa were invited of course. Arthur stayed at home as well with Mary so close to term."

That was a relief.

Their rooms were grand if a little old fashioned, but they had the latest amenities. A commode, bowl and jug for washing and a bath that could be filled by the servants. Georgina had the butler designate a hand maid for Sylvia and a footman for Charlton.

Dinner was announced by the strike of a loud gong that could be heard throughout the house and the happy couple made their way down to the large and imposing dining room. The table was enormous, with Henry sat at one end opposite the rosy-cheeked and tired-looking Mary at the other. Georgina sat near to Mary with Sylvia opposite and Charlton at Henry's right hand.

Beth had to keep a straight face. It was just so old fashioned. The rather ancient butler commanded the first course to be served. A footman stepped forward with a large tureen and a maid ladled soup into bowls; another placed the bowls in front of the diners. It was all very proper, and the servants were all in livery. The soup was leek and potato and well-seasoned. It was followed by a fish dish of trout and horseradish cream.

"Where do you get the trout? Surrey isn't renowned for its trout streams," Charlton asked.

"Stimpson, where does the trout come from?" Henry almost bellowed at the elderly butler.

"The River Nadder in Wiltshire, Sir. The cook's sister works for the Earl of Pembroke and the river passes through his lands. The fish are caught and shipped alive to us."

"Aah, George Herbert's place," Henry said knowingly. There was a pause and then he said almost defensively, "we do have some great course fishing here in Surrey and the Wey has brown trout. We have a fishing lake on the estate if you are interested. Mainly carp in there though as well as tench."

"Not a fisher," Charlton said, "more into hunting with hounds and shooting."

"Did you bring your guns?" Henry said hopefully.

"I did."

"Excellent, we can walk a few hedgerows in the morning and see if we can bag a pheasant or two."

At the other end of the table, Mary rolled her eyes when she heard that. "Henry does love to hunt; the kitchen is never short of game. It would be good for him to have someone to go out with."

"What do you do when he does?" Sylvia asked.

"The same as I do every day, needle point and crochet. I cannot do much else like this." She pointed at her prodigious bump.

Sylvia's heart fell, she would have loved to go with Henry and Charlton but in this house, it was obvious the women were expected to stay at home.

Back in their room.

"You are cross," Charlton said.

"I'm not," Sylvia snapped.

"Sounds like you are to me."

"Why do women put up with being treated like that?"

"Like what?"

"Being expected to be the little lady, stay indoors and supply the heir.'

"Aah, you want to join the shoot."

"Hmmph."

"Not all parents are as progressive as yours. In fact Lord Martin and Lady Caroline are probably way ahead of their time when it comes to that."

"I can probably shoot better than Henry."

"Who would be mortified if you did and probably very embarrassed."

"You sound like my mother."

Charlton laughed.

The next morning was trying. Beth was expected to spend time with Mary and Georgina. She was struggling with needle point and making a bit of a hash of it. Mary noticed and smiled.

"It's not for everybody you know," she said.

"Father always said I was a bit of a tomboy. Mother died two years ago but even before then I wasn't interested in needlepoint or sewing."

Mary smiled again, her cheeks rosy.

"Why don't you two — OH!"

"What is it?" Beth said and went to her.

"My waters broke! The baby is on its way."

Georgina looked aghast at the spreading puddle on the wooden floor then promptly fainted.

Beth looked around as she heard the thud as Georgina landed on the floor and rolled her eyes to heaven. She went to the bell pull and tugged it. A servant girl arrived promptly.

"Get Lady Mary to her bed. The baby is on its way."

Once the servant was helping Mary, Sylvia went out into the hallway, grabbed the first servant she saw and instructed him to go and fetch the midwife. He almost fell down the stairs in his haste. She made Georgina comfortable and went to help Mary.

They undressed Mary and got her into her birthing robe and into bed. The midwife arrived a half hour later and took charge. Hot water and towels had already been ordered as they knew that was what was always needed. A footman was sent to find Lord Henry.

Six hours later

"Is it here yet?" Charlton asked when Beth joined him for tea.

"Not yet, the midwife says it will be here soon as it's pointing in the right direction and all seems normal. Whatever that is."

"Have you seen a foal born?"

"Yes of course."

"Same thing, babies have to come out headfirst."

"I know that, it's all the other stuff."

"That, I don't know anything about."

"Neither did I. This has been an education."

They sipped their tea and Sylvia ate a cucumber sandwich then they went for a walk in the extensive and beautifully maintained gardens and deer park.

"The deer are very tame," Sylvia said. "Look, there are white ones as well as the normal brown ones."

They stopped and turned towards each other as newlyweds do.

"We should let them see us exchange at least one kiss," Charlton said.

Beth inside cringed but Sylvia turned her face up to his and allowed the kiss on the lips. It wasn't that bad; he was a decent kisser. Not as good as Sebastian but not bad. She broke away and linked arms, holding him close. From a distance they looked the perfect couple. They ended the walk at the stables to check on their horses. Melody chuffed a greeting and looked for an apple which Sylvie gave her.

"It's a good job you don't know my name," Beth whispered in her ear.

Bedtimes were more challenging. Modesty demanded that she cover up and they couldn't do anything about sharing a bed. He got a glimpse of her legs when she adjusted her thigh daggers in the morning.

"You have very nice legs," he said. Do you always wear those?

"If you have only just noticed then you aren't much of an agent," she teased. "Yes, I do. They were a present from my godfather."

"The one in St James."

"Yes, that one."

She was dressing in her riding habit as today was the day of the hunt.

"Aren't you worried they will fall out while you are riding?"

"No, they have loops to hold them in the sheaths."

The hunt was gathering at the Saddler's Arms Inn a couple of miles away and the hack over to it got their mounts nicely warmed up. The horse men and women were gathered outside and taking a stirrup cup of punch. Charlton led them through the horses to the Hunt Master and introduced them.

"Glad to have you, you will go with Samuel, my son." He looked around, then shouted, "Samuel! Here!" A young man walked his horse over. "This is the Right Honourable Charlton Manning and his lady wife."

Samuel greeted them, he was an affable chap and called a server over to get them cups.

"You will be riding in the fifth position after the gentlemen and lady members."

Hunt etiquette demanded that there was a strict riding order:

Field Master

Ex-Masters, Masters of other Hunts, by invitation of the Master

Gentlemen and Ladies with colours

Gentlemen and Lady members

Visitors and Guests with their sponsors

Juniors with colours

Juniors

There were dozens of other rules from what should be worn to how you rode in relation to other riders. Breaching any of the rules was seen as extremely bad form and would get you barred from the hunt.

The huntsman blew his horn and the hounds started to bay. They moved them out, the whippers in, keeping them in a pack, down the lane to the first field. The riders followed.

"Here we go," Samuel said, and kicked his horse forward.

Beth was riding astride for the hunt. Some women stuck to side saddles, but she wanted to jump as Melody was a fine hunter and Sylvia rode that way anyway. Once in the field the hounds accelerated to a run crisscrossing the ground as they looked for a scent.

A hound bayed that it had found one and they were off! They cantered across the field and then had a choice. Around through the gate or over the jump. Beth chose the jump; Sylvia would have too, but right then Beth was in charge. She kept her distance from the horse in front as it had rained overnight, and the ground was muddy, even so the odd clod hit her.

Coming into a fence the horse in front refused the jump and skittered sideways into her path. Melody answered to her knee and bridle beautifully and swerved to avoid the hapless horse and rider, changed legs, and launched herself over the fence. Beth could hear Charlton shout, "Yoohoo, Sylvia! Well ridden!"

At the end of the hunt, they were all tired, dirty, and happy. They hadn't caught a fox but following the hounds had been exhilarating and the jumps had been challenging. Two riders had fallen. One suffered a broken collarbone, the other just got muddy. All in all it had been a good day. There was to be a hunt ball that evening which they would attend.

Sylvia put on her best dress, a vision in lilac, made sure her auburn roots weren't showing, and applied makeup. Her biggest fear was that someone that knew her would be attending and she would be recognised. They made a fine couple as they descended the stairs to the ballroom on the ground floor.

They danced and then it happened, a girl came up to her and said, "My goodness for a moment I thought you were Bethany Stockley, daughter of Viscount Stockley. You do look alike apart from your hair colour." It was Lady Gillian Tamworth.

"Do I?" Sylvia said with a decided West Country lilt to her voice.

"Yes, you could be sisters!"

"I must meet her, where does she live?"

"Her father has estates in Cheshire and Dorset as well as a house in Grosvenor Square. He came up from nothing and married a baroness. He is a commodore in the navy."

"Did he? New money then."

"Absolutely! It's rumoured he is in trade as well."

"What? How common," Sylvia said.

"Friends with the king and all."

"Really."

"Bethany is really nice though."

"Is she?" She was saved from further revelations by Charlton arriving with a plate of food.

"Bethany Stockley?" he said as Lady Gillian told him as well.

"I heard she was a red-haired vixen who was as deadly as her mother and father. He, by the way, fought a duel for his wife's hand when they first met, and she fought a duel with a man who slandered her in the stock market. Sliced him up good and proper," Charlton said.

Lady Gillian visibly shuddered. "Bethany is rumoured to be a proficient swordswoman, but why she studies that, I will never know. Anyway, she was seen at the easter ball with a major of the Rifles, the fourth son of Shaftesbury."

They both knew she was referring to Sebastian but shrugged as if they had no idea who she was.

To Russia

Preparations complete, the happy couple embarked on the packet Andromeda for St Petersburg. The season was turning from autumn to winter and this would be one of the last ships able to reach the city before the ice closed in. Sylvia had become accustomed to Charlton and was more comfortable dressing in front of him, although she drew the line at being naked.

Being the more experienced agent, he continued her education with hints, tips and advice.

"You need a bit more shadow under your cheeks to highlight your cheekbones," he told her while she was dressing for dinner.

It is amazing how a little makeup can alter the shape of one's face, Sylvia thought as she applied a tad more. Her face looked a little more – haughty and sharp than it did normally and with the change of colour of her hair she hardly recognised herself. It was all part of getting into character. Satisfied she donned a bonnet and the two walked to the dining room. Luckily, they didn't need to go up on deck to do so as they had left the North Sea and entered the Denmark

Straits where the temperature was a balmy fifty degrees Fahrenheit and dropping as they went into the Baltic.

Dinner with the captain was a formal affair. One dressed appropriately, sat straight at the table, sipped one's wine decorously and ate daintily. One's husband was expected to hold conversation with the gentlemen leaving you to prattle with their wives.

There was an interesting couple. He was Austrian and a junior aristocrat being the third son of some duke or another and his wife was Hungarian by birth. They had been in England on a diplomatic mission and were now heading to Russia.

Lady Zorra was elegant, blond, with startling blue eyes, and intelligent. The other two women on the ship didn't speak English

"You are on your honeymoon?" she said by way of starting a conversation as Sofia was being shy. Her voice was rich and almost musical.

"We are," Sofia said a little breathlessly.

"A time to enjoy and discover."

"Discover?"

"The joys of being with your husband."

"Oh," Sophia said and blushed. "Is that something we should talk about?"

"Women talk about it all the time."

"They might where you come from but I've never heard them talk in England."

Zorra laughed. "I think the Austrian court is rather more open about such matters."

"You are Austrian?"

"I am Hungarian, my husband is Austrian. What will you be doing in St Petersburg?"

"We will be visiting the sights and have an invitation to visit the court."

"You are aristocrats?"

"My husband is the son of a baron."

"And you?"

"My father was a merchant, a very successful one," Sylvia said, head held high.

"Aah, I see. Is your father still alive?"

Sylvia blushed.

"An indelicate question, I apologise."

Sylvia looked down at her plate and sighed. "He became erratic in his dotage, and my aunt committed him to bedlam."

"I am sorry but that happens sometimes, my uncle lost his mind when he aged and couldn't remember anything except his childhood."

"It was horrible. It was like he died inside, but his body was still there." A single tear ran down her cheek; luckily her makeup was proof to that.

"We will be visiting the court as well," Zorra said, changing the subject.

"You will?" Sylvia said, brightening.

"Yes, my husband is a diplomat and has business to discuss."

"Have you been to the court before?" Sylvia asked excitedly.

"I have."

"What's it like?"

The rest of the meal was filled with scandalous revelations of the goings-on at the court that had Sylvia alternatively giggling and shocked.

That night in bed they compared notes.

"Lord Florian is a highly intelligent man and also quite resourceful, I believe. His father is in the inner circle of Emperor Francis who is burdened with running the German Confederation. They are apparently a troublesome bunch, always ready to fight over the slightest disagreement. He is ostensibly in Russia on a trade mission but there is more to it than that. I think he is there to make sure the Russians and Hungarians remain allies. Did you get anything from Lady Zorra?"

"Mainly that the court is a cesspit of sexual intrigue, apparently a hangover from when Peter III was in charge before Catherine the Great. Some of her tales were scandalous. She did let it drop that Tsar Alexander doesn't spend much time in St Petersburg, preferring to stay increasingly in Taganrog. She describes him as a liberal, introvert and shy. I will let her befriend me. She seems to want to take me under her wing."

"That's good, an ally will be useful."

"That's what I thought."

The next day, wrapped in a fur coat and hat Sylvia and Charlton ventured up onto the deck. It was overcast, grey and choppy. None of which bothered Beth as she was used to sailing. Sylvia however had to hang on to her husband on the rolling deck. Florian and Zorra joined them.

"I am glad to see you are well wrapped up," Zorra said to the two of them. She was dressed in a silver grey wolfskin coat that fell to her ankles and a matching fur hat. Her hands were gloved, and she had a wolfskin muff. She exuded elegance and wealth.

Sylvia wore a mink coat with fox fur collar and mink hat with a matching muff. The temperature had dropped to close to freezing. Her feet were the only part of her that were cold. The ship was powering along under pretty much full sail. Beth cast an eye over the way the sails were set without thinking.

"Have you sailed much before?" Florian asked, noticing the way her eye swept from fore to aft.

"No, this is my first sea voyage," Sylvia said. Beth cringed.

"For a moment you looked like you knew what you were looking at."

"I was trying to understand why some sails are further around than others," she improvised.

"You will have to ask the captain about that as I have no clue how to sail."

"My father had dealings with merchant captains, and I would go with him to Bristol sometimes. I would go on the ships in the dock but never under sail."

"Do you speak Russian?" Zorra said.

"When we decided to start our honeymoon in St Petersburg, I started to learn some. I can speak French and

Latin." That was safe as most young ladies of wealthy families would learn those.

"I can teach you some," Zorra said, "it will make the trip go faster."

The two wandered forward leaving the men to chat.

"What shall we start with? What do you know?"

"Privet, which is hello. Dobroye utro, is good morning. Kak vashi dela? Is, how are you? Spasibo, is thank you."

"Greetings and polite replies. Let us try naming some objects."

Sylvia was an attentive student, and the time flew by. She learnt a few new words but acted the student to perfection.

"You are a fast learner," Zorra said after three days of lessons.

"My tutors said I had an aptitude for languages."

"You were tutored at home?"

"Yes, Mama, when she was alive, had ambitions for me to marry well and she believed a good education would further that."

"Child, your mother was right as a man of means and power must be supported and aided by his wife. What does your husband do?"

"He will run the family estates when we return. His father is ageing, being sixty years old now. His family are aristocrats but the estate has been shrunk by the need to pay inheritance tax."

Zorra knew all about that.

"Your hand brings wealth?"

"I am the sole heir to my father's fortune. My aunt negotiated a very favourable marriage."

"Well then, you must be sure that your dowry is safe, as your fortune is now your husband's."

"Oh, I know all about that. That was why my aunt negotiated the terms of the marriage. My dowry is managed by Coutts bank, the bank of the king."

"And the rest of your fortune?"

"Daddy is still alive, although in a bedlam. I will not inherit until he passes. His business is being managed by his long-term factor, Mr Earnest Race, who will continue to manage it after he dies. My husband is happy to leave it as it is as the profits are substantial and will aid the development of the estate. He has many ideas on how to improve the land and the way it is worked."

Zorra sensed a core of steel in the young woman before her and liked it. The lessons continued and their friendship grew.

They crossed the Baltic as winter closed in. Making port as the first ice started to appear. The happy couple took a carriage to a lodging house on the edge of town near to the Winter Palace where the Russian court would move to soon, as Moscow was just too cold. As the coach moved away from the port they were struck by how downtrodden and miserable the workers looked.

"The surfs in Russia are more like slaves than free men. They have no choice but to toil," the driver told them. "Catherine the Great even enslaved many of our own people to build her palaces."

"Oh! That is dreadful. Has it always been like this?"

"Russia is a big country, with many people. The problem is they can only farm to survive or move into the city and work as cheap labour. The aristocracy is far removed from the people."

They passed what looked like a policeman and the driver stopped talking.

Snow was falling as they pulled up at the front of a large house which was more like a coaching inn than a lodging house.

"This is the place," the driver said and got down to help unload their baggage. The porter who came out of the door neither smiled or acknowledged them. "Go in, he will see to your luggage."

Inside they were greeted by a pretty girl behind the desk.

"We have been expecting you. Grand Duchess Catherine sent a message telling us to reserve rooms." The girl seemed impressed by the connection to the tsar's sister. King William I of Württemberg and Duchess Catherine were deeply concerned for Alexander. His health, both mental and physical, had deteriorated over the years and because of their family ties, the court would not talk openly in front of them. The king had been awarded an honorary Grand Cross of the Bath in the United Kingdom in 1815 for his contribution to the downfall of Napoleon. He was related to King George and had close ties to Wellington and George Canning and had asked for their assistance.

They were shown to a luxurious suite of rooms.

"No bath," Sylvia noted. She turned down the cover on the bed.

"Ugh, bed bugs!" she squeaked as she saw a black dot moving rapidly across the sheet to hide in the dark under the cover.

Charlton looked then pulled back the cover completely. A half dozen of the nasty little bugs were revealed. He swept them into his hand and threw them in the fire where they popped as they exploded.

"There will be more."

Sylvia cringed.

Dinner was a beetroot soup called Borscht, followed by a stew that was introduced as Stroganoff. The waitress was a pretty young girl who exuded a sort of sadness, something she noted in all the staff. Their host and his wife were stern taskmasters, and the wife was especially demanding.

"Is all of Russia like this?" Sylvia asked Charlton.

"If it is then we already know the root of the problem. They treat the staff as little more than surfs."

"We should take a walk and see what the rest of the city is like."

That night Sylvia chose a nightgown that reached to her ankles and wrists and made sure it was laced up tight around her neck. She wore a sleeping bonnet which covered her hair. It was unattractive but at least offered some protection from the bed bugs. Even so she woke up scratching bites on the exposed flesh.

They breakfasted then wrapped up warm to take a walk. It was lightly snowing outside and looked very pretty. As they strolled, they observed the people. There were a lot of soldiers and sailors as well as civilians bustling around on their daily business. The soldiers were in groups of four and obviously patrolling the streets. The sailors were making the most of some shore time. Everybody avoided the soldiers.

The shops were open and as they walked by them, they checked the goods for sale. The bread was dark and only one type was available. They watched a woman go in and buy some. The baker took her money, cut the end off a loaf and gave the shorter piece to her. She took it, holding it as if it were precious and scurried off.

They came upon a church that was being built. Poorly dressed men laboured, carrying roof tiles up ladders for the craftsmen to fit. Charlton stopped at the edge of the site and spoke to a well-dressed man. Sylvia stayed back as she had noted women kept themselves to themselves.

Charlton returned, took her arm and led her away.

"The labourers are slaves."

"Captives?"

"No, peasants. The tsar made a law allowing his own people to be enslaved for the construction. So much for his liberal values."

Sylvia was shocked, "I knew that Catherine the Great did that to get her palace built but had no idea the practice continued today."

"Apparently it is considered to be normal practice. The tsars may be said to be asset rich but cash poor so that is the easiest solution."

"And what about the rest of the peasants?"

"Uneducated and extremely poor. To be fair, Alexander came to the throne with good intentions to improve the lot of the peasants, but the sheer magnitude of the task defeated him."

A uniformed man approached them, "Show me your papers."

Arrogant and rude, Sylvia thought.

Charlton presented their papers including the letter of invitation to the court. She examined the man and decided he must be an officer.

"What is your name?" she asked, giving him a wide-eyed, admiring gaze.

"Alexander Abramovic, Captain of the Tsar's Guard, at your service, Lady Manning." He clicked his heels as he returned their papers.

"Your uniform is extremely smart, and the hat makes you look so," she drew in an admiring breath, "imposing."

The captain stood even straighter. "If there is anything I can do to assist please let me know."

"Will you be at the court?"

"I have the honour of having duty there."

"I look forward to seeing you again then." Sylvia fluttered her eyelashes at him over her shoulder as Charlton led her away.

"You were coming on a bit strong, why?" Charlton asked.

"As a guard he will be almost invisible to the members of the court, and they will say things in front of him that they wouldn't if anyone else was present. He should be a font of information."

"So, you will seduce him?"

"To an extent."

The Tsar's Winter Palace

A palace flunky arrived to take them to the Winter Palace. It was ornate and the horses had plumes of feathers on their harnesses. They had an escort of four cavalrymen mounted on black horses. People gave way as soon as they saw it and some even dipped their heads. The coach driver was a taciturn fellow who said nothing. The flunky was a chatterbox.

"You are guests of the grand duchess. It is such an honour to meet you," he started and talked without seeming to take breath for the entire trip.

The palace was impressive. It was designed by the Italian architect Francesco Bartolomeo Rastrelli in the Elizabethan Baroque style.

"It's huge!" Sylvia gasped as she took in the seven hundred and five by ninety-eight-foot building shining in white and green.

It was definitely very impressive from the outside and even more so inside. Catherine the Great and successive tsars had bought in whole collections of art and the walls were covered in paintings by all the major artists.

The massive frontage wasn't the whole palace, it was in fact, built around a courtyard and had around a hundred rooms a floor.

"You will be staying on the first floor near to the grand duchess's rooms."

The flunky, who's name she still hadn't caught, led them up the Jordan staircase. To say it was ornate did not do it justice. It was magnificent with gold covered bosses and scroll work on the walls. Worked in the finest white marble the staircase rose up four flights through the entire height of the palace. Bordered on the outside by pairs of blue marble columns and on the inside by a carved marble balustrade. Light shone in from fine clear glass windows. The ceiling was painted with an enormous mural depicting heaven.

They entered a corridor which was as richly decorated as the rest and shown to a suite of rooms that overlooked the inner courtyard which were paved.

"Guests get the lesser view," Charlton laughed once they were alone.

"The grand duchess's rooms overlook the palace square."

"Nice but can't people just look in the windows from there?"

"I suppose they can."

The first floor was in actuality a raised ground floor with a semi-basement level below where the kitchens and servants resided.

Their baggage arrived, carried by a posse of servants all dressed in fine livery. The smell of body odour was strong. Sylvia looked for a bathroom, there was none. She found a commode and a bowl with a jug, but that was about it. They had servants allocated to them. A pair of girls to take care of Sylvia and three footmen for Charlton. They were expected to eat in their rooms when they were not invited to dine at functions. The food would come from a separate kitchen that was shared by the apartments in that wing.

They had settled in when there was a summons from the grand duchess for tea. The door was answered by a liveried servant who was simultaneously haughty and servient. The haughtiness came from being the servant of a high ranking noble and therefore not a surf. The servility came from knowing his place. In other words in his world he was at the top of the tree but was aware that his tree was dominated by another much bigger one.

They were shown into a drawing room. It was immediately apparent that France was the dominant decorative influence.

Louis XIV and XV furniture, wall hangings and fabrics that would not be out of place in Versailles.

The duchess, in a voluminous dress complete with an elaborate headpiece smoking a foul-smelling cheroot, reclined on a chez lounge. They curtsied and bowed.

"Welcome to Russia," she purred in English. Her voice was deep and sensuous. "Canning said you were a young couple, with an exceptional amount of experience between you. I did not expect you to be quite so young."

Beth raised her head and looked at her proudly.

"He confided in me. I know your true identities Chaton and Archer. How is your father, Lady Bethany?"

"You may call me Beth and he is quite well thank you."

The duchess inclined her head in acknowledgement but said, "I will stay with Sylvia if you don't mind. It will avoid mistakes and the chance of being overheard. Your father has somewhat of a reputation, do you follow in his footsteps?"

"I did to start with, but I am making my own path now."

The duchess chuckled, a rich throaty sound.

"And you Mr Fitznorton, you come from the old blood. Will you be comfortable in court?"

"Quite, my Lady. I have been extensively schooled."

"Excellent." She turned to Beth.

"As you can see the fashions here tend towards the pre-revolutionary French styles. I expect you two will cause quite a stir, which is good because they will be so busy looking at your clothes, they won't see what you are really doing."

"Are there any individuals we should pay particular attention to?" Archer said.

"We don't know, that is why you are here. Someone is promoting an ultra-liberal doctrine to play to the masses."

"The same ones who sent Catarina Lesniak to Britain?" Beth said.

"Probably, is all I can say at this time. Her parents are here by the way, but I do not think they knew what she was involved in."

A servant approached with a tray of tea. The cups were Chinese porcelain of the highest quality. So thin they were translucent and delicately painted with the duke's coat of arms. When he had left the duchess continued.

"My brother has become a recluse. That allows the court's usual rivalries to get out of hand, I want to know what is going on and stop it."

"Can I ask, why did you ask the British to help?" Alain said.

"Apart from not being able to trust our own agents after the Catarina incident, King George is my husband's uncle. George Canning is an old friend. I like to keep these things in the family."

"Georgie is my godfather," Beth said.

"I know, so you are family too."

That afternoon they attended the court in the throne room. Even though the throne was empty the court had assembled, and an official read out messages from the tsar. It looked like something out of a history book to Sylvia who was wide eyed in wonder at the colourful dresses that were heavily embroidered and brocaded. The women wore a kind of headpiece that was a crescent worn toward the back of the head that supported a lace veil that hung behind the head. They were mostly elaborately jewelled.

"I simply must get one of those!" Sylvia gushed to her husband.

She needn't have worried, her mane of brown hair with the jewelled headpiece the king had given her was attracting admiring glances. Added to that she was at least half a head taller than most of the women in the room and her husband was taller than almost all the men.

The Russian court had a reputation for rather loose morals, and it didn't take long for Charlton to start receiving signals by fan. He ignored them as the duchess was introducing them to the more important courtiers. Sylvia was being watched openly by several men. She was glad that Beth's mother had made sure she was fully equipped. She smiled inwardly at the split in her personality. Beth watched while Sylvia played the naïve newlywed. Observing the players around her and evaluating who looked interested, who looked offended and who looked calculating.

It was when she was introduced to Count Nikolay Nikolayevich Novosiltsev, who was the minister of foreign affairs, that her interest was piqued. Catarina had been working for him as part of Russian Intelligence before she went rogue. Sylvia curtsied as he bowed, his lips just brushing her hand. He was tall by Russian standards at five feet six inches, the average being around five feet three to four. Sylvia was taller than him by an inch or so and they both wore shoes with a bit of a heel. She saw a handsome older man of about fifty years, fit looking, immaculately dressed with a hard cast to his eye despite his welcoming smile. He wore a grey wig that had a ridge down the middle which looked rather odd as he had black sideburns sticking out below it.

He, in turn, evaluated her. He knew who and what she and Charlton were. He saw a young woman, tall, elegant, beautiful but promising to become even more so. He noted the headdress and would bet good money it was lethal. He wondered what other weapons she had hidden about her person. He knew of her father and was friends with Admiral Senyavin, who had met him in Portugal.

They were joined by another aristocrat, Prince Victor Kochubey, Minister of the Interior. He was the third person who knew who they were.

"My dear Catherine, let us meet later in your apartments and discuss what needs to be done," he said softly, "in the meantime why don't you two circulate and see who is who."

They asked after Lord Florian and Lady Zorra but were told that they had gone to meet the tsar in Taganrog, Sylvia was sorry not to have seen Lady Zorra again as her observations would have been inciteful.

They moved out into the room and were soon engaged in conversation. They listened more than they spoke. Many just wanted to meet the newcomers and find out who the Russian-speaking English were. The explanation that they had a distant kinship with the duchess satisfied most but one man probed them more closely.

"How is it that the grand duchess invited you to St Petersburg?"

Sylvia gave the explanation they had been given while Beth checked the man over. He was dressed all in black with none of the decorations seen on many of the men's collars. His starched collar stood high up his neck and a white cravat, or neck wrap, covered his neck to his chin. He had pallid skin like he never went outside, and he had a suspicious look on his face at all times. His name was Ivan Lebowski and he came from Odessa.

"What do you do in court?" Charlton asked.

"I am the secretary to Minister of the Interior."

"Prince Victor? He is such a nice man, we met him earlier," Sylvia said empty headedly. They chatted and he let her know he enjoyed riding.

Another couple who came across as very friendly, caused Beth's antenna to quiver. They were brother and sister, Philip and Motina Kristopas who were Lithuanians. Sylvia latched onto Motina as they were of an age and soon the two were giggling over a wicked observation by Motina of an elderly count.

"Did you see the scornful way Philip looked at the courtiers?" Beth said later in their rooms.

"Yes, he looks as if he despises them. Anyway, I found out he worked for Prince Victor on the liberal Privy Committee when Alexander tried to reform the government," Alain said. "We need to find out what his current political inclination is."

"Motina told me he still works in the Interior Affairs department, but she didn't seem to know what he does."

The clock on the mantelpiece chimed seven.

"It's time to visit the duchess."

They crossed the corridor and knocked on her door which was opened so fast it made Beth jump. They were ushered inside and led to the drawing room where Count Nikolay and the duchess were sat chatting and sipping glasses of champagne. The count stood and greeted them with a bow which was returned.

"Viktor will be here directly," the duchess said, "he is in a meeting."

Beth and Alain expected him to enter through the main door and were surprised when a bookcase opened, and he stepped into the room.

"Secret passages?" Alain said.

"There are many. Initially designed so lovers could meet without being seen. Many have fallen into disuse, but the palace is riddled with them."

"No one knows Victor and I are here," Count Nikolay said.

"What about the servants?" Charlton asked.

"They are all from Württemberg and can be trusted as none speak Russian," Catherine explained.

A footman entered and announced something in German.

"Come we should move through to the dining room, dinner is ready."

The table glittered with silverware and crystal glass. A soup was served a moment after they had sat.

"What were your impressions of the court?"

"The women seem to be rather promiscuous," Beth said.

"Yes, they see sex as a way to climb the social ladder," Nikolay said.

"Some just jump beds for fun," Catherine said. She looked at Alain. "I expect you have had invitations already?"

"Yes, and one rather direct one from Countess Annita."

"Aah yes, she is the worst of the lot." That was all Nikolay would say.

They moved onto the next course, fried perch.

"Did you notice anything else?"

"There are definite factions which seem to be based around people who support the reforms, those who do not and those who think they should go further. I suspect there is also a group who are militantly inclined towards more radical changes."

"Do you have names yet?"

"We have but would like to dig a little deeper before exposing them."

"That is fair, but as soon as you have any evidence you must report it," Victor said.

When they returned to their room they started searching for secret doors. This involved searching any internal walls whose thickness couldn't be determined, paying particular attention to cupboards and bookshelves. The wall between their apartment and the next was the most obvious choice and it also happened to be in the bedroom.

Beth stood back and looked it over. There was a large mirror opposite their bed. She cocked her head to one side and twirled a strand of hair as she looked at it. Alain watched her. She looked damned attractive.

"You know you—"

"Shhhh," Beth said, lost in thought.

She was trying to figure out what was jarring her eye. She moved to her right a couple of steps.

"Hmmm."

She stepped forward. The mirror was about six feet tall with a dark wood frame. To either side it had carved and gilded columns topped in gilded cone motifs. Above the glass the frame extended up into a panel with a classical peaked roof. The panel was decorated on either side with gilded urns and two horns of plenty in the centre.

"That's not quite right," she said and reached up to the left-hand horn. She turned it and there was a click. The mirror swung out on hidden hinges.

"Ta da!" She smiled and bowed to Alain.

"Oh! Well done," he applauded then went to his trunk and opened one of its many secret compartments. He removed a small, shuttered oil lantern that had a polished reflector and lit the wick.

"Shall we explore?"

"After you." Beth grinned after retrieving a similar lantern and a pistol.

The passageway was narrow, cobwebby and dusty.

"Not been used for some time," Alain said.

"Ugh, no it hasn't," Beth said, using the pistol to brush away a large, inhabited cobweb. There was a scurrying sound.

"Rats," Alain said.

A couple of yards from the entrance on the opposite wall Beth noticed a teardrop-shaped wooden plaque. She brushed aside the cobwebs and moved it to one side. She looked through the hole to see a Russian lady undressing. She recognised her as the wife of one of the junior ministers. She had shed her dress and petticoats and stood in not much more than a see-through chemise and stockings. She went to the bed and lay down. A man joined her, he was not her husband.

"What did you see?" Alain whispered as she closed the eyehole.

"Nothing you would be interested in, just the wife of the minister for buildings entertaining another man."

"We should keep notes of who's having sex with who?"

"Voyeur!"

"It might be relevant!"

"Maybe."

They traced the passage which descended to pass under the corridor. At the bottom there was a crossroads. To the left and straight ahead it showed signs of use and to the right no use.

"The duchess's apartment is straight ahead, and I bet that Victor's and Nikolay's are down that way," Alain said.

Beth started making a sketch of the passages on a wad of paper she had in a pocket in her dress. They took the passage to the right that ran under the corridor. They found another spy hole and found it was high up in the throne room on the floor below. They discovered another three before they came to another junction. All looked down into the throne room and it was amazing how much could be heard.

"The acoustics are perfect. You can hear almost everything," Beth whispered.

"A previous tsar must have been a little paranoid." Alain chuckled.

"They all are."

They spent until the early hours mapping the passages. They discovered Victor and Nikolay's apartments, witnessed a number of illicit liaisons and numerous secret doors that hadn't been opened in decades. They got back to their apartment covered in dust and cobwebs.

"What I need right now is a bath," Beth said.

"I know what you mean. I feel decidedly grubby."

Beth made a decision and rang the bell for a servant. It was three in the morning and the servant arrived bleary eyed and sleepy.

"Get me a hogshead barrel that has been cut in half and twenty buckets of hot water."

"What, Mistress?" the confused servant said.

Beth repeated the order.

"Do you think they will do it?"

"I bloody well hope so as there is something wandering around under my dress."

It took an hour but a pair of footmen carried in the half barrel which could hold eighteen gallons. A train of servants carried buckets of hot(ish) water.

"Put the water in the barrel."

They filled it to about eight inches from the top.

"That is enough. Now leave."

Beth didn't wait for Alain to leave as well and stripped before stepping into the barrel.

"Aaahhhh!" she sighed and then looked over her shoulder.

"You still here? Well pass me that soap."

Alain had the water after her.

They slept in the next morning and the palace was alive with speculation on what the strange English couple were up to. The duchess chuckled when a servant told her what had happened. This would shake up the place.

Suspects

Without a doubt they were the cleanest couple in the palace. Sylvia also wore a delicate perfume. Her hair shone as she had brushed it over a hundred strokes and was styled to fall across one of her shoulders in the style of the ancient Greeks. It had the desired effect; men were falling at her feet. Charlton also wore a subtle cologne, and it was apparent he too had a distinct lack of passengers of the vermin variety. The ladies were crowding ever closer.

To the disappointment of many, Sylvia chose to single out Ivan Lebowski. She found him and treated him to a beaming smile.

"Ivan! I am so pleased to see you."

"Why?"

"I love to ride and you said you did too. I was wondering if you had a spare mount and could take me out."

"Your husband?"

"Oh, he will stay here."

Charlton picked out Motina Kristopas and her brother. He was frustrated by his attraction to Beth, exacerbated by the view of her naked the night before, and was setting out to establish a closer relationship with Motina. For entirely professional reasons of course.

Ivan took Sylvia to a livery stable close to the palace. She was swathed in furs and wore a riding habit underneath. The horse she chose was a well-conformed, sixteen-hand, grey mare with a slightly skittish temperament. He rode a rather dull fifteen hand bay gelding.

He led her across the Palace Bridge to Vasilyevsky Island. Recent snow muffled the horses' hoofbeats and the occasional flake fell gently to the ground. They rode side by side close enough that their knees occasionally bumped. They rode past a building site and Sylvia looked at the peasants with sympathy.

"Those poor people, having to work in these conditions."

"They are surfs. If they do not work, they do not eat and their families starve."

"Is that just?"

"It is the system." Ivan sounded bitter.

"Then I would question the system."

"You do not understand Russia. It is massive and it is ruled by just one family. There are many ethnic groups and only the upper classes receive any education at all unless you are extremely lucky."

They left the bridge and passed through a town laid out in a grid pattern.

"The town was originally supposed to have canals like Venice which is why the roads are all straight. It is still part of St Petersburg."

The homes here were mainly for the upper middle classes and if that is all you saw you would believe everything was wonderful. However, Sylvia knew better and once they left the town and into farmland, she noticed farmhands working outside.

"What are they doing? It is too cold to dig. The ground is frozen."

"They are digging up turnips and carrots. They will feed some to their animals and take some for themselves."

"Do they have meat to go with them?"

"Not all the time."

Sylvia spluttered, outraged.

"That's not right!"

"Damn right it isn't but it's hard to change things."

"Ivan isn't part of any conspiracy. He is too meek to risk doing anything like that," Beth said to Alain that night. "How did you get on with the siblings?"

"Motina and her brother despise the tsar and his government with a passion. They are convinced that the people deserve better and the only way to get that is to overthrow the ruling elite."

"How did you get them to tell you that?"

"Not them, her."

Beth rolled onto her side so she could look him in the eye. He blushed.

"Did you bed her?" she asked evenly.

"I…"

"You did!" She rolled to her back and laughed.

Alain looked confused. When she recovered, she said, "Sylvia would be as mad as hell."

"I let her seduce me. Her brother sat outside the room keeping watch."

"In this bed?"

"No!"

Beth raised her eyebrows in question.

"On the chaise lounge."

She laughed again.

"Then Sylvia has a damn good excuse to run her through."

"But…"

"Oh shush, I'm not going to do that. Sylvia is going to go to her crying that she thinks her husband has been unfaithful."

"Asking for sympathy?"

"Yes, and while she is at it will reveal that she thinks the plight of the peasants is upsetting her and she wishes she could do something about it."

"They know we have money, maybe they will try and get some out of us for the cause."

"I think I need to visit their rooms. See if I can find anything."

"When?"

"Tomorrow afternoon when you are entertaining her."

"I am? I mean, alright. Will you be able to manage on your own?"

"Can you?"

Deth crept down the passageway. She had taken a broom to it one night and swept away the cobwebs and dust on the floor so as not to leave obvious tracks. She followed her map to the secret door in Motina's room. *Thank you for the randy Russian tsars,* she smiled. A quick peek through a spy hole and she could see the room was empty. She sprung the catch on the door, it had been recently oiled by Alain as had the hinges, so swung silently open at a slight push.

The bedroom was untidy. Dresses were thrown across the bed and chairs and stockings lay on the floor. Motina had obviously been in a hurry and couldn't make up her mind what to wear. Beth crept across the floor to the door to the salon and listened.

"Your sister is shagging the Englishman again?" an unknown voice said.

"Yes, she enjoys it, if the moans from the last time were anything to go by," a disgruntled Philip said.

"It's all for the cause," the voice laughed.

"What if his wife finds out?"

"She won't, and we will use it to blackmail as much money as we can out of him. Let him enjoy dipping his wick in your sister's honeypot for the moment and then we will confront him."

Beth smiled; she wouldn't have minded discovering sex with Alain but that was out of the question now. In any case, she was going to save herself for Sebastian. If she could.

"You had better get over to their apartment and make sure they aren't disturbed," the voice said.

Beth peered through the keyhole in the door but all she could see was it was an older man with grey hair. After he left, she started her search. She was methodical, starting at the bottom drawer of a chest of drawers and working her way to the top, making sure that there was nothing stuck underneath the drawers. Chests were rummaged and secret compartments checked for.

She completed Motina's room and moved to Philip's. She didn't rush, letting her training and instincts guide her. There was a travel trunk in a closet which at first glance appeared to be empty. She checked it all the same and voila! She found a false wall. She used a slim jim to work the wall loose and carefully laid it to the side. Inside was a single folded paper. Beth removed it and took it to the light of the window to read it.

It was in Russian, in plain language and, at first glance, a shopping list. She decided to copy it and, after replacing the panel and making sure everything was as it should be, left the room via the secret door and went to the duchess's rooms.

"Sylvia, an unexpected pleasure." Catherine was not surprised in the least that she came in via her bookcase.

"Good afternoon, Lady Catherine. May I borrow your desk for a moment?"

"Feel free, what do you have there?"

"A paper, I need to copy it and return it to where I found it."

Catherine watched over Beth's shoulder as she created a perfect replica of the paper. Once she had completed it, she took the original and disappeared into the passageway to return a few minutes later.

"Where did you find this?" Catherine said. She sat at the desk, studying the copy.

"In a hidden compartment in a travel trunk."

"Why would anyone wish to hide a shopping list?"

"That is what I thought, so it must be something else."

Catherine gave up her seat to Beth who sat and studied the paper, twiddling a lock of hair as she thought. Catherine watched her and smiled; she was quite exquisite. Suddenly Beth jumped to her feet.

"I need the original," she said and disappeared again.

Beth removed the original again and compared it with the copy. The paper was the same and the copy was as good a forgery as you could make. She folded it precisely the same and creased it to make it look as close to the original as she could. Job done she put everything back where it belonged and went to the bedroom door. Just as she was about to open it voices came from the corridor.

It was Philip and Motina!

She moved fast and just got the secret door closed when Motina came into her room. Beth watched her through the spyhole. Motina threw herself on her back on the bed. She was laughing.

"And what is so funny?" her brother asked from the doorway.

"I have never had so much fun setting up a blackmail in my life."

"I heard," he growled.

"He is a fantastic lover. If we weren't going to use him, I might consider keeping him."

"If his wife finds out you might be in trouble."

"That mouse? She is no threat."

Back in the duchess's apartment, Beth asked for a candle. She lit it and carefully warmed the paper with it.

"I knew it," she said as writing appeared.

"What does it say?" Catherine asked.

"It's a list of names."

"Contessa Catarina Lesniak's name is crossed out."

"Let me see."

Catherine read them.

"Please copy it," she said and handed the paper back before tugging the bell pull to summon a servant.

"Please find Prince Victor and ask him to attend me. Tell him it is a matter of some urgency."

Prince Victor was there within fifteen minutes.

"Catherine, Sylvia, what is so urgent that you disturb my afternoon nap?"

Beth handed him the copy of the list of names that she had made.

"Do these mean anything to you?"

Victor scanned the list, his eyes widening as he did.

"There are several known dissidents here and a couple of suspected ones. Where did you find it."

"Hidden in a chest in Philip and Motina Kristopas's room in a hidden compartment in their travel trunk."

"I had my eye on them but didn't know they were this deep in with the extremists."

"She has been screwing Charlton with a view to blackmailing him for funds. It appears it's not the first time she has done it."

"My oh my, what a wicked web she weaves," Victor said in English. He paused, then asked, "What would Sylvia do if she found out?"

"Sylvia learnt to fence as a young girl as she was an only child and her father treated her like a son. She would challenge the bitch to a duel."

"Can you fence?"

"I can use a sword, or any other weapon."

"Expertly, no doubt. Our intelligence on Miss Kristopas is that she can also fence. I doubt she would refuse a challenge."

Beth returned to their apartment to find Charlton fast asleep in a chair. She kicked him on the foot to wake him.

"Oh! You are back. Did you find anything?"

"Yes, a list of the members of the extreme liberals which includes some prominent names and some known dissidents."

"I assume you have shown it to the powers that be. What do they want to do next?"

"Your indiscretions are going to come to light," Beth said and sat on his lap. "I am to cut your balls off and challenge the bitch to a duel," she said sweetly.

Alain's eyes widened.

"Metaphorically of course where the balls are concerned," she laughed.

Murder Most Foul

Beth and Alain were preparing to visit the court when a scream split the air.

"What the hell was that?" he said as he pulled on a jacket and headed towards the door. Beth pulled on her dress and urged the servant girl to do up the laces at the back quickly so she could join him. She emerged from their apartment to a chaotic scene.

The doors to the duchess's apartments were open and there were people crowded around it trying to see in. She pushed her way past them into the drawing room. Charlton was knelt beside the chaise lounge beside a prone and very dead-looking duchess. A shocked, sobbing servant girl stood to the side.

Beth didn't hesitate, she shut the door on the gawkers, locked it and sent a servant to fetch Victor. She then went to the body and gently moved Alain out of the way.

Catherine's face was frozen in a rictus, her back arched and arms rigged, her hands clawed. There was a cup on the floor. Beth picked it up by the handle, careful not to touch the bowl or what was left of the contents. She sniffed it, and the scent of bitter orange was prominent.

There was a knock at the door she unlocked it to let Prince Victor in with two men in long coats.

"She is dead?" he asked, somewhat unnecessarily.

"Poisoned," Beth said.

"Any idea with what?"

"Strychnine is my guess. Served in a cup of bitters to disguise the taste."

"She took a cup every day for her health."

"Well, someone knew that and used it to administer the poison." Beth sat back on her heels and looked at the duchess sadly. "The question is who would want her dead?"

"Anyone on that list of names. She was known to be standing in her brother's stead."

"It's a declaration of war," Charlton said.

"They think they have chopped the head off the serpent, now would be a good time to purge the problem but I would have to get Alexander's approval," Victor said.

"No, it is too soon. I think it is time for me to challenge Matina to a duel. Then when I have finished with her you can have your purge."

Victor nodded and ordered the body to be wrapped and taken to the mortuary. Beth asked that she talk with the doctor before he performed any kind of autopsy and was told bluntly that a person of the grand duchess's status did not have an autopsy. She frowned and asked that the body be held in a cold place until she could examine it. She also asked for the cup to be carefully wrapped and preserved as it was. Then she took Charlton by the arm and became Sylvia.

The court was buzzing with the news, and they were looked at with suspicion. A messenger was dispatched to carry the news to King William who was in Württemberg. Charlton looked very sheepish and guilty about something, which was immediately noticed by the gossip-hungry courtiers. No announcement about the grand duchess had been made yet.

Matina and Philip entered and Matina looked at Sylvia with a smirk which turned into a smile as Sylvia approached. Sylvia was smiling sweetly until she stood directly in front of her.

"I was hoping to see you. You see, Charlton talks in his sleep and I couldn't help but notice you being mentioned over and over again. I mentioned it when he woke up this morning and at first he denied knowing you at all but then his conscience won over and he confessed. You seduced him."

"It wasn't hard, I am a real woman not like you, you simpering little wallflower," Matina hissed.

"Wallflower? Well you will find this one has thorns."

And with that she slapped her across the face hard enough to almost knock her over.

"I challenge you to a duel," Sylvia cried in an impassioned voice.

The audience of courtiers gasped.

Matina laughed through the tears that ran from her eyes,

"Women cannot duel! You stupid bitch."

"Actually, that is not true," Count Nikolay said as he walked up to them. "It is perfectly legal for women to duel; do you accept the challenge?"

Sylvia looked at him and he winked surreptitiously.

"I do." Matina leant closer and hissed, "I will cut you into little pieces."

"So, you choose swords?" Sylvia said.

"I do."

Sylvia turned to the count, "Is there any reason why the duel should not be fought immediately?"

"If you have seconds, then no reason at all."

"Charlton will be mine."

"And Philip will be mine."

Charlton stepped forward and asked Sylvia, "Will you withdraw your challenge?"

"No."

He turned to Matina with pleading eyes. "Will you apologise?"

"Not for you or anyone."

Sylvia beckoned to a servant standing by the door and he came forward with a long case, stood between them and opened the lid. Inside were two exquisitely made small swords with gilt knuckle guards inlaid with enamel.

"Choose your weapon. They are French and identical," Sylvia said.

Matina didn't look quite so confident now as she picked up one sword then the other. They were identical and she chose one at random. Sylvia picked up the second. Count Nikolay had paced off a fighting circle and had a servant mark it on the floor with chalk. The courtiers gathered around, excited by the prospect of a fight.

Sylvia strode to the centre and toed a line drawn two sword lengths from a second line. Matina followed her in. The count acted as Master of Ceremonies.

"To the death or until one is unable to fight," Sylvia said.

Matina nodded in agreement.

Sylvia could hear bets being placed and she allowed Beth to step forward.

"En guarde!" the count commanded.

Beth took her stance. Right foot forward, knee bent. Matina matched her, but while Beth had her left hand behind her back she had it curved up behind her at head height.

"Engage."

Matina flicked her sword point forward, Beth retreated and parried. She stepped back assessing her opponent. She played the practised amateur, sticking to the forms. On that basis Matina believed she was the better swordswoman. She toyed with Beth, who let her, staying just out of reach. Beth tried a deliberately clumsy attack which Matina parried using croisé. Beth responded with a feint and a coupé which got her inside Matina's defences. The point of Beth's sword slid home in her left shoulder. She disengaged and stepped back.

"First point to me," she said. The audience applauded.

"En guarde!" the count commanded calling the combatants to the line.

Matina snarled something under her breath and took her stance, blood trickled from the wound staining her dress. Beth changed stance to that of a knife fighter. Feet shoulder width apart, knees slightly bent, weight over the balls of her feet, both arms held in front.

"Engage."

Matina attacked as Beth knew she would with a wicked compound attack. Beth parried the intended kill strike aimed at her heart and pirouetted allowing Matina's momentum to carry her past her. As she did Beth punched her in the temple with the knuckle guard. Manita hit the floor and slid a couple of feet before coming to rest on the edge of the circle. The crowd was stunned and then erupted into applause.

Sylvia feinted.

Beth cracked an eyelid as she was put down. She and Manita had been carried to an anteroom by their seconds. Philip was tending to Matina's wound; she was still unconscious. Charlton and the count stood over her. She opened both eyes and grinned at them.

"Help me up," she said in English to Alain, then turned to the count. "Is this room secure?"

"I have guards posted outside."

"Is there a dungeon?"

"No, but there is a cellar."

"Can you have those two moved down there? We need to interrogate them."

The count understood.

"I can do better. I have a hunting lodge outside of the city. We will move them there. No one will hear anything."

Beth gave instructions of how she wanted the siblings treated.

It was a clear starlit night. The ground was covered in a thick layer of snow and the moon just peeked over the horizon. The two-horse sled skimmed over the ground; the occupants wrapped in furs. It was delightful. Beth breathed in the crisp cold air and blew out a plume of breath steam. Tonight would be long and difficult and she didn't relish what she was about to do, but it had to be done.

It took an hour to reach the lodge. It was a strongly built wooden cabin a couple of hundred yards inside the edge of the forest. Smoke drifted up in a solid vertical column from the chimney in the still air. Light glowed from the windows. The sled pulled up at the door and they went inside.

The siblings stood barefoot on the cold stone floor, hooded with their arms tied behind them. Ropes were looped over a beam and tied to their wrists forcing their arms up into a painful position which also forced them to stand on the balls of their feet putting strain on their legs.

"How long have they been there?" Beth asked.

"About an hour," one of the attendant soldiers said.

A groan escaped from Philip's hood.

Beth stepped up to him and felt the pulse in his neck. It was strong and regular. She repeated the exercise with Matina who swore at her.

"Now, I will ask you some questions. If you answer them to my satisfaction, you will be let down. If you don't then things will get progressively worse until you do."

"Fuck you," Manita spat.

Beth nodded to the soldier who pulled up the rope an inch causing Manita to groan in pain.

"What is your name?"

Neither answered.

She nodded to the soldier again. Both ropes were pulled in a couple of inches.

"What is your name?"

"Philip Kristopos."

"Shut up, you fool!" Matina cried.

"It's only my name, she knows that already," Phillip sobbed.

Beth moved over to Matina and placed her thumb over her wound and pressed. Manita screamed.

"What is your name?"

"Fuck you!"

She pressed harder. Matina screamed louder.

"Matina, Matina Kristopos!"

"There, that wasn't so hard, was it?"

"Where do you come from?"

"Lithuania."

"Where in Lithuania?"

"Vilnius."

"Excellent, I hear it's a beautiful city. Do you want to see it again?"

"Yes," Manita sobbed.

"We will have to arrange that."

"What about you, Philip? Do you want to see it again?"

"Yes."

"What is your mother's name?"

"Gabija," Philip said.

Beth was handed a note by a clerk who was transcribing what was said.

"Liar." She kneed him in the balls.

Philip screamed. Alain took over.

"Save yourself the suffering and pain. She is quite ruthless, you know."

"Leva her name is Leva."

Manita was crying.

"Hear that, Manita is crying. You don't want her to cry or be hurt anymore, do you?"

"No."

"Did you murder the duchess?"

"What? No, we didn't!"

Beth prodded Manita's wound making her cry out.

"We didn't have anything to do with that!" he cried out in anguish.

"Do you know who did it?"

"No, it was nothing to do with us."

Beth did it again.

"Stop, oh, stop. Please we didn't murder her."

Alain believed him.

Beth wanted to be sure and pulled up the rope holding Matina's arms. She screamed in pain.

"She doesn't believe you," Alain whispered in his ear, "I do but you need to give her something to make her stop."

"I think it was Gregor."

"Gregor who?"

"Gregor Kaminska, he is a servant in the palace and a contact."

The count spoke to one of his men who left immediately.

"Now let's talk about the list of names you had hidden in your trunk," Beth said.

The next morning Beth visited the mortuary where Catherine was lying. It was as cold in there as it was outside. She examined the body looking for puncture marks. There were none, so she could eliminate a dart. She then checked for bruising, especially around the neck. She had talked to her maid and knew that Catherine didn't take strychnine for medical reasons.

The next step was to analyse the cup which she took back to her rooms. As there was no known way of detecting strychnine, she decided to test it on a rat which she'd caught using a drop cage supplied by the servants. She made a solution of the residue in the cup and soaked a piece of bread in it. She fed that to the rat. It died after convulsing horribly for a minute or two.

Back at the lodge she informed the count and the prince of what she had found.

"My conclusion is that she was deliberately poisoned with strychnine. The murderer may still have some in his or her possession."

"We haven't found any in the Kristopas's room or Gregor's. Gregor has been questioned and admits to being an accomplice of the Kristopas's but denies any involvement in the murder. He was in the kitchens at the time and for the two hours before, so has an alibi."

That left them at square one.

Investigation

Beth sat in the window of their apartment looking out over the inner courtyard of the palace. Alain watched her from a chair. She idly twiddled a lock of her hair. The weak winter sunlight shining on her.

"Anything interesting going on out there?" he asked.

"Hmm? Oh, nothing really. I was just thinking."

"About the murder?"

"Yes. Who would want to kill Catherine?"

"Maybe the question is, *why* would someone want to kill Catherine? If we knew that, then we could narrow down the search."

Beth turned to face him and propped her chin up on her hands, elbows on her knees.

"We know how. Strychnine poisoning in her daily cup of bitters. I suppose we need to know why and who to solve this."

"That's what I said."

"But I said it better."

"If you say so." Alain smiled at her serious expression.

"The palace was sealed off after the murder and no one is allowed to leave, except us that is. So, the murderer must still be here."

"Do you have a copy of that list of names?" Alain said.

"Yes, on the desk over there."

Alain stood and retrieved it, sat down and looked through it.

"Philip told us the list was of the core members of the ultra-liberals. They are heavily influenced by the writings of Voltaire and Charles Fourier. Especially his ideas on Utopian Socialism. He has visited here and talked to people in secret."

"That man gets in everywhere. I may have to find him and do something about him," Alain snarled.

"You can't burn all of his books. His ideas are public now."

Alain turned back to the list.

"Are any of these in the palace?"

"Not that we know of."

Prince Victor stepped out of their bedroom.

"Good afternoon," he said.

"Hello, Victor," Beth said, she had given up using honorifics in private. "We were discussing the list."

The prince sat in a chair and crossed his legs. It was noticeable that he was carrying a pistol clipped to his belt. He saw Beth look at it.

"All my men are armed. You should be too."

Beth smiled and a pistol and silver dagger appeared in her hands from under her dress. Alain opened his jacket to show a pistol in a holster slung under his arm.

"I might have known." The weapons disappeared. "We have been through the list and have agents tracking down those on it."

"You know where they all are?"

"We know where they all should be. We will know where they are when our agents find them, and the reports come in."

"Has the news of the duchess's murder got out yet?"

"No, we sealed the palace as soon as it was discovered, and no one has been allowed out."

"I want to talk to Catherine's staff," Beth said.

"We already did that," Victor said.

"I might have better luck?"

He looked at her. She seemed focussed and determined.

"Alright, come on."

He didn't use the passages but took her straight across the corridor. The two guards on the duchess's door snapped to attention.

The servants were gathered together. One spoke Russian and translated for Beth.

"Who made the bitters?" Beth asked.

A young maid stepped forward.

"What is your name?"

"Hilda, Ma'am."

"How long have you been on the duchess's staff?"

"Three years, Ma'am."

"Are you the only one who prepared her bitters?"

"I did it every day, Ma'am. She liked the way I prepared it."

"Show me where you prepared it."

Hilda showed her to a kitchen where all the food prepared in the apartment was done.

"Where are the bitters kept?"

"In here, Ma'am." Hilda opened a cupboard. "Oh, they aren't there!"

Beth was making notes and looked up. "Prince Victor, have your men removed the bitters?"

Victor stepped into the kitchen and the maid immediately lowered her eyes.

"No, nothing has been touched. Why?"

"Because they aren't where they should be."

Beth returned to the sitting room and questioned each and every servant about their length of service and what their job was. When she had finished, she turned to the prince, "Can you bring in two guards and fetch Alain for me?"

Victor, intrigued, did as she bid and when the guards and Alain were present, she said, "You two keep these people here. Alain, help me search their rooms."

They searched every inch of the servant's quarters even checking the floorboards for hidden compartments. They found nothing. Beth sat on the last bed and pondered the problem, twiddling the lock of hair as she did. A draft made her cold and she looked for the source. A window was cracked open.

Why would anyone want the window open? It's cold enough in here without letting the outside in.

She went to it and saw that the latch had been closed on the wrong side of the hasp.

"Somebody closed this window in a hurry," she said out loud and opened it. Like the rest of the apartment the room was on the ground floor and overlooked the palace square. The ground was covered in a layer of fresh snow. *Well, that doesn't help.* Then she noticed an indentation. She climbed out of the window and used her knife to gently move the fresh snow away. It was a footprint. She measured it using her hand's span. *A man's.* She looked for another, that close to the palace there was very little pedestrian traffic.

There was another slight indentation a pace away and a third beyond that. Then they disappeared as the snow was thicker away from the walls. She sighted along the line of the steps. They headed for the construction site where a column and statue of Tsar Alexander was being erected to commemorate the defeat of the French in 1812. She walked over to it.

"Beth! Where are you going?" Alain called.

"I'll be back in a moment!"

The column had been raised and the statue stood proud above it, but the surround hadn't been completed. She scuffed away the snow with her foot and found a patch of sand. It wasn't frozen and looked loose. She knelt and carefully scooped it away. Her fingers brushed something hard. With the care of an archaeologist digging a fragile artifact she excavated around it to reveal the bottle of bitters.

Another rat died in the cause of forensic science. Beth had found the murder weapon.

"It gets us closer. We now know how the poison was administered. Someone put it in the bitters, probably the night before, so that when Hilda made the tea with it the duchess got the fatal dose," she told Victor and Nikolay.

"Good God, so the culprit is one of the servants!" Victor said.

"It would seem that way."

"But they are all trusted retainers."

"So, it would appear."

"You have doubts?"

"I could open that window from the outside with no trouble at all, and added to that the footsteps only went away from it. That suggests that whoever buried the bottle left and didn't come back."

"But you can't be sure of that," Alain said.

"No, but it is a possibility we have to keep in mind."

Beth stood and walked to the door, "Now I want to interview the male servants again."

"Who sleeps in this bedroom?" Beth asked the assembled men.

Two stepped forward.

"Are those your only shoes?"

"Yes, Ma'am," they said in unison.

"You are Carl and you Peter. Am I correct?"

"Yes Ma'am," they chirped together again. Carl was in his twenties and Peter probably in his forties.

"Take off your shoes and give them to me."

The men looked at each other and Peter shrugged and took off his shoes followed by Carl.

Peter's shoes were too small, he was a short man with small feet. Carl's were more of a match to the footprints outside. Beth measured it with her span. It was close. She examined the sole and the join between the upper and the sole. They had been recently cleaned and polished, but something might be lodged in the gap. There was nothing she could see.

"I will take these for closer examination."

Carl looked surprised and said, "But what am I to wear?"

"You don't need shoes. You aren't going anywhere." Beth walked out of the room.

Back in their apartment she placed a sheet of paper on the desk and tapped the shoes on it to dislodge anything caught in the seams or joins. Then she took a stiff bristled paint brush and thoroughly brushed the joint between the upper and the sole. Tiny pieces of something accumulated on the paper. She went to her trunk and retrieved a magnifying glass. She could see dust and bits of fluff but no sand. Peter was not her man.

She sat back in her chair. Alain, who had watched her at work, said, "Any luck?"

"No, Peter is probably not our man. Whoever planted the poison came in from outside, hid in the apartment until the kitchen was empty, then poisoned the bitters. Once he heard the scream, he recovered the bottle and exited through the window."

"That's a workable theory."

"It is and now we have to prove it. Let's have another look at that window."

Alain brought along the magnifying glass and examined the catch closely. "There are marks here. Looks like someone used a slim jim or thin bladed knife to try and close the latch after they left."

"So our culprit broke into the room and hid. When the coast was clear, crept out and put the poison in the bitters."

She paused, a frown creased her brow. "How did they know that the duchess took bitters every day?"

"They must have been told by one of the servants. They were the only ones who knew she did it."

Beth strode out into the sitting room where the servants were gathered. She separated the women from the men and said quietly, "Did any of you talk to any men from outside the palace?"

"I talked with the man who supplied the goods for the kitchen," the cook said.

"Ingrid, isn't it?"

"Yes, Ma'am."

"Did he speak German?"

"Yes, with a Westfalen accent."

"Don't you think that's strange?"

"He said he was a local but had spent time in Stuttgart."

"What was his name?"

"Vladimir."

"What did you talk about?"

"The duchess, what she ate. So, he could make sure she got the best stuff."

"Vladimir has disappeared. We have sent out his description and set up checkpoints," Prince Victor said.

"If he left straight after the duchess died then he could be anywhere," Alain said.

"Not quite," Victor replied. "Travelling across country is extremely arduous this time of year and extremely dangerous as the temperature drops dramatically at night. I think he may have taken to a ship."

"Have many left port since the duchess was killed?" Beth asked.

"None, it is iced up."

Beth grinned. "Then he's probably still in the city or on a ship."

The army were called in and a house-to-house search was carried out. His known associates were arrested and questioned. Every ship in the harbour was thoroughly searched. They found smuggled goods and contraband but no sign of Vladimir.

What would I do? she thought. A light came on in her mind. "I would hide in plain sight," she blurted.

"What?" Alain said.

"I would change my appearance and hide in plain sight if I was Vladimir. He knows there is no sensible way out of the city, so he stays put. Changes his name and appearance to someone everybody looks past."

They went through the passages to Prince Victor's apartment, checked he was there through a spyhole and knocked on the secret door.

"To what do I owe this pleasure?" he said as they followed him through to his sitting room.

"I have a question," Beth said.

"Ask."

"Do your soldiers search the slaves?"

"Slaves? Why would they search them?"

"Because if I was Vladimir that is how I would hide to avoid detection."

The prince looked surprised, then thoughtful.

"That isn't as mad as I first thought. Who knows what he looks like?"

"The cook, her assistant and Cedric the footman in the duchess's staff. There are probably more in the palace staff."

The prince had his men find everyone who had met Vladimir and several platoons of soldiers, the servants, and Beth and Alain were marched out of the palace into the city where they split up to cover as many sites using slaves as possible.

Five men were identified as potentially being Vladimir and were brought to the palace. Beth asked if she could examine them.

"Tell them to strip."

"Madam, is that appropriate?" the officer in charge asked.

"Tell them to strip," she repeated slowly.

"Yes, Ma'am," he said, warned by the cold grey of her eyes.

The men lined up, most just stood there but one covered his genitals.

Beth drew her dagger, causing a surprised gasp to come from the officer. Alain stood in the background with his hand on his pistol butt and watched as she stepped forward to the man.

She pricked his hand with the point.

"Modest." She ran the point up over his stomach and across his chest. "Well fed." She reached up and cut a lock of his hair from his head and then another from his beard. She took the samples to a table where she had left a leather case. She opened it and took out a pair of test tubes and three bottles. She put the hair in the test tube and added distilled water from one of the bottles. She swirled it then strained the fluids into the second test tube. She held the tube up to the light and satisfied with both the quantity and the lack of particles added two drops of nitric acid. She swirled the mixture then added liquid from the third bottle the mixture immediately turned cloudy.

"He has used silver nitrate to dye his hair and beard. That is Vladimir." To prove her point she stood in front of him and said, "Move your hands." He didn't move so she moved her dagger to his belly and pushed. His hands moved, fast, to grab her arm. She was ready for that and brought her knee up hard.

Vladimir lay on the cold ground clutching his bruised balls. Someone was rubbing his back and speaking softly. When the pain subsided, he sat up and was immediately dragged to his feet and his hands bound behind his back. No one made any attempt to give him clothes. The young woman with the knife stood to one side talking to Prince Victor.

They had cleared the table of the case and bottles and were attaching straps under the direction of a tall man. Servants arrived carrying buckets of water. The woman looked at him and gave an order, softly but with an air of expected obedience.

He was manhandled onto the table and his arms and legs bound down, a strap placed across his forehead and tightened so he couldn't move his head. Her face appeared above his.

"Hello again," she said sweetly, but her eyes gave away the lie. "I am going to ask you questions and you are going to answer truthfully. If you don't, you will have to face some consequences. Let me demonstrate."

A cloth was suddenly held on his face crushing his nose, he opened his mouth to breath. Water was poured on the cloth and ran into his mouth; he choked. He was drowning.

It stopped. He coughed and gasped for breath. Her face reappeared. "That was unpleasant wasn't it." She looked thoughtful for a moment. "You know I could have chosen the Captain Morgan method. Do you know that? I would tie a cord around your genitals and hoist you up by them. Now I am going to ask some questions and you are going to answer or you will get the same treatment again only for longer. Do you understand?"

"Yes," he said, he remembered the drowning sensation vividly.

"What is your name?"

"Vladimir."

"Vladimir what?

"Vladimir Roscovic."

"You are Russian?"

"Yes."

"Where were you born?"

"Novgorod."

"What is your father's name?"

"Peter."

"What was your mother's name?"

"Tatiana."

"Do you have brothers or sisters?"

"No."

"Where was your father born?"

"Minsk."

"Are your parents still alive?"

"No."

"Where were you born?"

"Minsk."

As soon as he said it he knew she had caught him in a lie.

"Now you have lied to me. First you tell me you were born in Novgorod, then Minsk." She moved away.

The cloth came down on his face and the water started to flow.

He tried to hold his breath, but the water kept coming until he had to try and breath. The water got into his lungs, he was drowning, and it kept coming. Suddenly it stopped and the cloth was removed.

Her face appeared again.

"Now, where were you born?"

He coughed up water and she wiped it away gently with a cloth.

"I don't want to have to do this, you know, but you are forcing me. You will tell me everything eventually so get this over and done with and your suffering will end."

His resolve not to say anything kicked in, Beth saw it in his eyes. The cloth came back.

"Vladimir told us everything eventually. He was tough and it took several hours to break him."

So, what do we know?" Prince Victor said.

"He put the poison in the bitters. He got the poison from a man he knows as Konstantin. She was killed because she was seen as propping up Tsar Alexander and known to be trying to track them down. They also wanted to make a grand gesture."

"Did he know any of the people on the list?"

"He was a frequent attendee at meetings where he met several of them."

"Interesting."

"Konstantin wasn't one of them. He described him as middle class."

"So, no direct link to the group."

"Not through him but he told us that Catherine's influence was discussed, and the general opinion was that she should be removed."

"That's enough for me. We will shut them down."

"Can I suggest you wait for a little while?"

"Why?"

"So we can attend the next meeting, which is next week on Tuesday."

"How will you get in?"

"Philip Kristopas will introduce us."

Secrets

Philip was nervous. He had been coerced into helping the British bitch and her husband if that is what he was. He knew them as Sylvia and Charlton Manning, but he had heard her called Beth. He didn't know if that was a pet name or what, but he had heard her call him Alan or something like that. Nevertheless, he would cooperate as they held his sister and Sylvia had promised in a whisper in his ear to carve her into little pieces and feed her to the palace dogs if he didn't cooperate. She had been so cold and matter of fact he believed her.

The three of them took a carriage from the palace across the Palace Bridge to Vasilyevsky Island, through the industrial zone and navy yards to a farmhouse on the edge of the built-up area. Light shone from the windows and several carriages were hitched to posts outside. He knocked on the door and a burly man answered it.

"Pushkin," Philip said. The door opened and they were admitted.

Inside, the living room had been cleared of furniture and people stood in groups talking. Philip walked over to a particular group and greeted them.

"Hello, Philip. Where is Matina?" A man with a goatee beard and moustache in the imperial style with the tips curled above the moustache itself.

"She has a cold and is too ill to go out," Philip said and then indicated Sylvia and Charlton. "May I introduce friends from Britain, Sylvia and Charlton Manning."

"Welcome, my dears. Do you have an interest in liberal philosophy?"

"We were members of the group with Catarina and listened to the philosophy of Charles Fourier and his vision of a utopian socialist society," Charlton said.

"You knew Catarina?"

"I had made her acquaintance. Sylvia knew her better than I."

"I met her a number of times at her house. It was there she was killed," Sylvia said.

A small crowd gathered as people overheard what she said.

"What happened?" a man demanded.

"I wasn't there that night, but Sylvia was," Charlton said.

"We were at one of our regular meetings when it was unexpectedly raided by the police. I was talking to Catarina at the time when the door burst open and armed policemen came in."

"They shot her?"

"They didn't have their guns raised to start with and we just stood there open mouthed at the invasion of our privacy. Then somebody fired a gun and, suddenly, many of the police drew theirs and fired back. The next thing I knew she had slumped to the ground; a bullet through her heart. I think I heard someone say it was a ricochet."

"Why did the police raid the meeting?"

"They claimed that some of the members had been in Birmingham agitating the workers."

"Had they?"

"Catarina and Charles had been in the midlands, so I suppose it is possible. In any case, Charles was accused of sedition and deported. They used his case to preserve the Aliens Act which was being opposed by the Whigs."

"The Whigs?"

"The liberal party in Britain. It was that we were discussing at the time of the raid. The members of the group were going to propose a split from the party to form a more socialist party."

"The raid could have been politically motivated?"

"I suppose it could, but I really do not understand politics. Could that happen here?"

"We are a peaceful, academic, group. We are not in favour of direct action, so why would it?"

Sylvia went to a table to get a drink. An elegantly dressed woman stood beside her.

"Poor Catarina is sadly missed. Her parents were devastated."

"She was a lovely person." The lie slid off Sylvia's tongue and she took a sip of her drink. "I was talking to a man in town and he was very angry about the way Russian society is organised," she said as if just remembering it.

"He should be careful, talk like that can get you arrested. Do you know his name?"

"I think he said it was Constantine."

"Konstantin. He was a member here, but he was thrown out for being too radical and militant. Strange that you should meet him."

"We were taking a walk past the docks, and he came out of a bar. He was somewhat worse for drink and berated us for being part of the bourgeoisie. Charlton told him flat that we were not Russian and certainly not part of the ruling class. Then some soldiers came by and he left rather abruptly."

"That makes sense. His family are middle class and comfortably off owning a fur trading company. He was never happy being the youngest son and got in with the workers on the docks."

"His poor mother, what must she think?"

"Olga Dimitrova is a tough one. She has four other sons that are doing very well thank you."

"I suppose every family has a black sheep."

The meeting was more of a gathering of intellectuals and only two of the names on the list were amongst them. The discussion about the tsar's liberal ambitions was discussed and it was clear that they felt that Catherine had put a brake on them. But there was no feeling that anyone wanted to assassinate her, they just wanted her to go back to Germany.

Sylvia and Charlton left, taking Philip with them and the next morning debriefed with Prince Victor.

"So you are saying they are mostly harmless?"

"No threat apart from their ideas which revolve around creating some kind of benevolent society where the state looks after everybody equally."

"And who rules that state?"

"Academics, they think rational thinkers are the only ones qualified. What is of more interest is that we can be fairly sure that the man we are looking for is Konstantin Dimitrova."

"I know his father. The boy was always a troublemaker but I am surprised he would go so far as to assassinate the duchess."

"He is the only lead we have." Beth hesitated: she wasn't sure the suggestion she was about to make was going to be acceptable. "I think that we could find out how big and how far reaching this radical group is."

Prince Victor looked at her, then rolled his eyes to heaven. "The young, they believe they can do anything. What is it you want to do?"

"Infiltrate the group, or at least get close enough that I can listen in on their conversations."

"Don't you think that's better left to my men?"

"That's the point! They are men, I can be almost invisible."

"You have a point. We did request your aid and so far you have been successful. What do you have in mind?"

"Sylvia and Charlton will leave St Petersburg to go to Moscow once the announcement of Catherine's death is made. I assume you won't be saying she was poisoned?"

"She died of natural causes. A consumption."

"There will be a new servant girl at the bar Konstantin frequents."

The next week a tired-looking, grubby, barefoot, girl walked into the bar on the docks and asked for a job. She was pretty under the dirt and got Ivan the owner's attention when she said she could dance.

"Show me," he said and started a beat on the counter.

The girl struck a pose, modest and shy, then her head came up and her eyes flashed. She tossed her head and pulled off the scarf that bound her hair. Rich auburn hair fell halfway down her back. Her foot stamped in time with the rhythm then she started to dance. It started teasingly; an invitation that avoided somehow being completed. As she danced, she kicked forward exposing a pair of very shapely legs. The dance became more intense, and increasingly provocative until it ended with her standing proud, her arms above her head, wrists entwined. She was breathing deeply and slowly relaxed back to stand in front of him.

"If you dance like that you will fill this place. You can serve tables as well. Go out back and see Anya. She will clean you up and give you something nice to wear."

Ivan had a friend, Dimitri, who could play the balalaika and he asked him to accompany Mila. The bar was half full when the time came. Dimitri started to play a popular folk song which the drinkers paid little attention to. Then Mila walked out into the room. She had a calf-length skirt with petticoats, a white linen blouse and a red shawl over her shoulders. Her hair had been washed and brushed till it shone. She strutted to the clear space that had been left amongst the tables. She stood, head held high, shoulders back, challenging every man in the room to look at her.

The balalaika fell silent.

A foot stamped a rhythm. The balalaika started a slow pulsing tune of loss. Mila started to dance, telling the story of the tune. The loss of her lover, her grief.

The tune picked up and she danced loneliness and searching until the final third where she rediscovered herself, a strong independent woman ready for a new relationship. Challenging the men in the room who started to whoop and stamp along with the beat. She finished with a pose, proud, strong, invincible. The men went crazy, and coins showered her feet.

The next night the bar was full, the word had gotten around, and as she served drinks men asked when she would dance. Three men sat in a corner and watched while she placed drinks at a particular table. She flirted with the men and one pulled her, laughing, onto his lap. She stroked his face and slid out of his arms when he reached forward for a kiss, staying just out of reach. Ivan smiled from behind the bar. She was worth her weight in gold.

Mila assessed the room after her dance. Customers were asking if she could dance again, and she knew Ivan would ask her soon. She talked to Dimitri and they decided on a faster gypsy dance. In the meantime, she went back to serving drinks.

She brought tankards of beer to the table in the corner. Alain sat there with two of the prince's agents. They exchanged a few words, and she went back to work. Beth made sure she got the area where Konstantin and his friends sat. She served the table next to them.

"They have announced that the grand duchess died of consumption," one said. "That's not what you told us.'

"They are lying to cover it up," Konstantin said.

"The men are waiting for a grand gesture to incite the workers," the third man said.

"Then we shall have to give them one," Konstantin said.

One of the men looked at her, she had been stood still for too long.

"All you do is talk," she said, "do you want more drinks?"

"Bring a bottle of vodka and glasses."

"The good stuff or the cheap stuff."

"The good stuff of course."

She returned with the bottle and four glasses. She waited for the payment.

Konstantin waited for her to bend over the table to pick up the coins and slapped her on the rump. "Are you dancing again?"

She grinned at him. "In a minute."

He left his hand where it landed.

"Come and see me after."

The next dance was wild. She strutted and teased and kicked, high showing her legs. She ended near Konstantin's table on one knee, hands hold high. She stood after picking up the coins, another landed at her feet. It glinted. It was full rouble. Konstantin grinned at her. She grinned back and batted her eyelashes at him.

"You and me would make beautiful music," he said.

"Would we?"

Ivan called for her.

"See me later," he said.

Ivan kept her busy and shooed the men out when the bar closed. She slept in a small room he provided for her, dressed in clothes he provided for her and ate food he provided for her. She was treated as his property. He let her keep less than half of the money she got from dancing, and she asked if she could go to the market. He gave his permission with a warning to be back by noon.

Alain was waiting at the market and as she went through a pile of cloth, he stood close enough to talk to her without seeming to be.

"They are disappointed with the announcement that Catherine died of consumption. It didn't turn out to be the grand gesture they planned it to be. Did you follow his friends?"

"Yes, they are all staying at a lodging house. The police did a routine visit, and it appears two are from Moscow and the other from Minsk. The rest of the men that he talks to in the bar are locals."

"They talked about the boys being ready to incite the workers if a grand gesture is made."

"They are planning one?"

"I think they might be. I need to get closer to find out. I think I am going to have to start a relationship with Konstantin."

Alain shuddered at what her father would say if he heard what she intended. He was wrong of course; Lord Martin knew that she had to do whatever it took to complete the mission.

"Be careful."

Alain faded into the crowd. She bought a length of red material, and some coloured threads then made her way back to the bar.

That night she danced again, only this time Konstantin was there on his own. He talked to Ivan who nodded after he passed over some coins. When Mila finished her second dance, he pulled her down onto his lap as she served him a drink.

"Ivan has given me permission to walk out with you tomorrow."

"Walk out?"

"Yes, we can go for a walk."

"That is all?"

"Yes, nothing more."

"Good, because I am not a prostitute," she said, giving him a 'don't even think it' look.

He met her at the bar and they walked out together.

"Is it true you turned up at the bar barefoot?"

"Yes, although it's much more comfortable walking in snow in boots."

"Why?"

"Why is it more comfortable in boots? Or why did I turn up barefoot?"

Konstantin laughed, "Barefoot."

"Because I had no shoes."

"Why?"

"Is that your favourite word?"

"I'm curious."

"I was orphaned when I was six when my family tried to move towns. They were killed by Cossacks near the River Terek. They took me and sold me to gypsies who brought me up as one of their own. I learnt to dance there and left the band when it passed St Petersburg."

"That explains your strange accent. I was wondering about that."

I have a strange accent? She made a mental note to address that.

He bought her some bangles at a stall in the marketplace. They were brass but shone nicely enough. They passed a building site.

"Those men are slaves?" she asked.

"Yes, either sold into slavery because of debt or because they are poor."

"It is disgusting that we Russians enslave our own."

"You don't approve of the way Russia is run?"

"I was a gypsy. We were driven out of towns by the ruling classes just because we wanted to trade or mend a few pots when the people were mostly pleased to see us. We would fix a pot for half the price of a smith."

"And rob the rich when they weren't looking," he added a little sarcastically. "The lower classes outnumber the middle and upper classes by millions, yet they grow fat on our labours," he said with passion.

She stopped and looked at him, her head tilted to one side.

"You look middle class to me."

"An accident of birth, I am for the lower classes."

She tucked her arm through his.

"Tell me more."

Fifteen yards away, close enough to get to Beth, if she got into trouble, but far enough away to not be noticed, Alain, dressed as a local, leaned on a wall and watched. He could lip read and smiled as Beth went to work. She flirted, letting Konstantin know she was interested without coming on too strong.

They moved along the row of stalls. Alain followed and made sure the other members of the cover team were in position. He wished he had M's Shadows, but they were with him somewhere on a mission. He had three men around the couple and another up in a church belltower watching with a telescope. They were all Prince Victor's agents and well trained by Russian standards.

As he followed, he noticed two men pacing the couple in the next aisle of stalls.

Now who are you? he wondered. He had a choice. Keep the full cover on Beth or detach a man to follow the pair. He made his choice and signalled the cover man on that side to follow them. In any case if they continued as they were, his man would still be in range if anything happened.

They moved out of the general market and headed to a livestock market a couple of streets away. Now things got more difficult. There were far fewer people to mingle with and they would have to drop back.

Beth spotted the two men and signalled Alain by moving her right hand behind her back and opening and closing her fist two times, followed by an open hand with her thumb across the palm. The fingers pointed to her left.

Konstantin was regaling her with a funny story about a bolting horse when they heard horses walking towards them; the sounds of their hooves echoing off the buildings. They turned to see who it was.

"Cossacks," Konstantin said.

Beth pretended to be afraid and moved into his arms.

"It's alright, they cannot hurt you here," he said and held her.

The Cossacks, mounted on their Steps horses, were dressed in blue, long coats, high leather boots and fur trimmed hats. Their torsos were crisscrossed by leather straps which held a rifle across their backs and a sabre at their side. They rode in pairs and forty of them passed by.

The two men shadowing them slipped into a convenient alley which was interesting. *Why don't they want to be seen by the Cossacks?* Beth thought. She also couldn't help noticing that Konstantin kept his face hidden behind her hair.

Alain was also curious. The two men had concealed themselves very rapidly once the Cossacks appeared. He would ask Prince Victor about that later. Beth was playing the frightened maid to perfection as the horsemen passed and now they were clear of them stayed very close to Konstantin. They visited the pens where horses were held awaiting sale.

"These are Dons, they aren't so big, but they can run all day." Konstantin said.

"I know, we had smaller versions that pulled our waggons." Beth petted a pretty grey mare. The trader approached and handed her a shrivelled apple.

"Are you buying?"

Beth fed the mare with the treat, enjoying the softness as the mare's lips stroked her palm. The horse's big brown eyes looked into hers and nuzzled her neck

She stroked her ears. "I wish I was. I would buy her in a heartbeat. How much is she?"

"She is worth all of fifteen roubles."

Konstantin let out a snort. "You will never get that for her."

The dealer gave him a very direct look. "What would you pay?" the word 'umnik' (wiseguy) hung unspoken in the air.

"I think she would go for, maybe," Konstantin looked her over, "nine."

The dealer laughed. "Last year maybe, but this year there is a shortage of good horses. She will sell for fifteen or close to it at the auction this evening."

Beth got back to the bar in time to work the lunchtime service and made contact with Alain who was at his usual table. She passed him a report written on a very thin piece of paper folded and concealed under his tankard.

"You saw me looking at a horse in the market?" she said quietly.

"The grey?"

"Yes, that's her. I want you to buy her for me at the auction this evening."

Alain managed to hide his surprise.

"How much should I pay?"

"I don't care, just buy her."

"It's your money," Alain said.

"Did you identify the two men?" Beth said changing the subject.

"Not yet, we are watching them."

"Mila, don't stand there chatting all day! There are customers waiting!" Ivan bellowed across the room.

Mila gave him a look and strolled across to the bar to collect the next order. Her walk was deliberately provocative.

"And don't think I can't throw you back out on the street," Ivan said.

"And lose all those customers I bring in?"

That evening she danced and even though she danced to the whole room Konstantin felt she was dancing just for him.

Beth slipped out of her room via the window and made her way across the rooftops. It was well into the night, and she dressed in her one-piece black overall, a hood covering her head. Konstantin lived in rooms on the edge of the docks district. His affinity for the poorer classes didn't extend to roughing it in one of their hovels. He had told her he had to be out of town for one night to attend a meeting. The prince was taking care that he was followed. She was taking the opportunity to search his rooms.

She got to the house having only stepped on the ground twice to get there. His rooms were on the first floor and she used a rope tied to the chimney to lower herself to a window.

A quick stroke with a slim jim opened the catch and she was inside. It was the kitchen. She closed the curtains and lit the oil lamps.

The kitchen was untidy but clean. He evidently didn't eat there as the kitchen showed no signs of use except for four glasses that were upside down on the counter by the sink. She opened the closest cupboard and found two bottles of vodka. One was half-empty.

Beth quickly searched the kitchen then moved onto the living room. There was a desk with a chair behind it and a bookshelf with a few books on the wall behind that. She checked the books.

Pushkin, Voltaire, Fournier, predictable. She shook each book and rifled through the pages to make sure nothing was hidden in them then turned her attention to the desk. The drawers weren't locked and took but moments to search. There was nothing of interest in them. On top of the desk was another leatherbound volume. She opened it.

A journal! The writing is awful, and only a rank amateur would keep one. She turned it to the latest entry after scanning some of the early ones. She read:

I must attend the meeting in Schlisselburg. The prison there holds many of our people and other opponents of the tsar. I will miss Mila. I will talk to Ivan about her again when I return. I will be a hero in the eyes of the people when the prisoners are released, and she will be pleased to take me as her husband.

Oh bugger, Beth sighed. She turned back through the journal and stopped when she saw a name she recognised – Catarina.

Catarina is going to go to Britain. The workers there are ripe for revolution now that they have a pig for a king.

So, she was a member of this group. Beth sat down and started reading the journal in earnest. Catarina was definitely a central figure as she was mentioned several times. The last was:

We have heard that Catarina is dead. Not only will I miss her personally, but the group will miss the inside information from the secret service she provided.

Will they indeed? Beth put the journal back precisely where she had found it. It was time to report in.

Prison Break

"So, you think they will try to break prisoners out of Schlisselburg Prison?" Prince Victor said after Beth gave her report.

"That's certainly what it looks like," Beth said.

The prince was in a dressing gown as Beth had gone directly to the palace after leaving Konstantin's room. She had entered his rooms from the secret passages, having used one that exited the palace in the hermitage. It was three in the morning.

"Do you know when?"

"I will try to get the date out of him when he returns."

"We never suspected Catarina was working with them. Did the journal say anything about what information she gave them?"

"Warnings when meetings were going to be raided, who was sympathetic at court or in the civil service. Things like that."

The prince looked troubled and spoke without looking up.

"Go back to the bar and get some sleep. My men will increase surveillance on all his associates."

Beth left how she had come, and the prince paced up and down the room. He pulled a bell pull and when a servant arrived looking sleepy said, "Get Gaskin here now."

Gaskin was his head of operations and a more ruthless individual you were unlikely to meet. He arrived in thirty minutes.

"I have received intelligence that dissidents are going to attempt to break their friends out of the stronghold at Schlisselburg."

"That agrees with rumours we have heard, but we had no concrete evidence. A squad of Cossacks has just arrived. Can I have permission to send them to Schlisselburg to reinforce the security force there?"

"How many?"

"Forty."

The prince thought for a moment or two. "Have them go there by a roundabout route and slip into the town at night. I don't want the dissidents to abort their attempt. We may not get another chance to round them up."

"Understood, Sir."

"I want increased surveillance on the ones we know. Are there any men undercover in the socialist groups?"

"No, the last one was killed in an accident at the foundry."

"Then we are reliant on the British girl," he sighed.

Mila waited patiently for Konstantin to arrive back. Ivan kept her busy and the patrons loved her. She was finishing the lunchtime service when his voice said, "There are better ways for a girl to live." His arms slid around her. She turned in their circle and kissed him.

"You are back. How was your trip?"

"Good, very good. Can you get away this afternoon?"

Mila looked over at Ivan who scowled at them.

"He's not in a very good mood."

"Then I will talk to him."

He went straight over, and Mila resumed clearing up. She watched out of the corner of her eye as coins changed hands.

"Meet me in the market at three o'clock," Konstantin said.

They ended up back at Konstantin's rooms. They sat on the bed kissing, and he was getting increasingly passionate. Beth had been taught the basics of seduction and how to set and close a honey trap. She hadn't expected to call on that training so soon but she started to put it to good use.

"Konstantin, stop!" she said and pushed him away as he started to fondle her breast. "I am a good girl and want to stay that way until I am married."

"Oh, Mila, we can do so much without going all the way," he gasped.

She looked down, there was a noticeable bulge in his trousers.

"Why should I marry you?" she said and let her fingers touch his thigh not far from the bump.

"I will be a hero when the revolution comes." He was sweating.

"How can that be?"

He boasted of his influence and key role in the people's party. How he was going to lead the group in a grand gesture that would inspire the lower classes to rise up and throw the aristocrats out of power.

"I don't believe it. What are you going to do?" Her fingers crept closer. He gasped and shifted his position, so they touched the swelling. She stroked it. He stiffened and went rigid.

"I will lead a raid on – no I cannot tell you!" His voice had gone up half an octave.

"I could go with you." She stroked it again.

"Argh, a raid on Schlisselburg Fortress! Oh my god!"

"Really? And I can go with you?"

"God! Yes!"

"So, when should I be ready?"

"Next month before the 23rd." She kissed him and stroked some more until he shuddered and relaxed.

"You didn't have to sleep with him?" Alain asked.

"No, nor get naked." Beth's expression remained neutral.

Alain left it at that, he could face her father with a clear conscience. Instead, he asked, "Is there any significance to the date?"

"23rd March was when the last tsar was assassinated." Prince Viktor said.

"I can see why they think that is a significant date," Beth said.

"He will take you with him?" Alain said.

"He will if the others let him."

"Let us know. In the meantime, keep him interested," Victor said.

Alain looked her in the eyes and took her hands in his.

"He is obsessed with you, Beth. Be very careful as that can turn to hatred if he realises he is being used."

"I will be. I want to get home with Polina."

"Polina?" Victor asked.

"Her new horse which she had me buy at the auction, cost me twelve and a half roubles."

"You will get it back." Beth smiled and kissed him on the cheek. "Where is she?"

"In the palace stables. How are you going to get her back to England?"

"She will be absolutely fine on the ship."

The meeting finished and Beth went to the stables. She was about to go to Polina when she saw a man walking across the yard. Something about him struck a chord and she slipped into the shadows behind a stack of hay. He walked through a patch of weak sunlight. It was something in the way he moved. A slight limp? No, he had the rolling walk of a sailor, but there he was dressed in a groom's uniform. Beth put the uniform out of her mind and concentrated on the way he moved and tried to get a glimpse of his face. He went into the carriage barn, and she slipped over to the door to see if he she could get a better look.

An arm clamped around her neck and a voice growled in her ear. "Now what are you doing here, little Mila, or is your name something else?"

She reacted without thinking, ducking her chin down inside the crook of his elbow, grabbing the arm and digging her nails in as she pulled down and twisted towards him. Her boot heel came down hard on his instep, her left hand dropped and clamped talon-like on his genitals.

He howled from the assault on his arm, foot and balls. The arm loosened. She slammed her head up into his face, mashing his nose. A stiletto appeared in her hand and was rammed up under his chin through the roof of his mouth and into the back of his brain. He was dead before his body hit the floor.

"Did you have to kill him?" Prince Victor asked, grimacing at the sight of the knife. "He is staff after all and you didn't know he was anything else."

"My training kicked in," Beth said, as if that explained everything. She looked at the dead man's face and twiddled a lock of hair. She frowned and lent forward. She pulled the knife out with a wet slurp and his face tipped forward.

"That's better," she said and looked at him carefully.

"I know him, he is one of the men that hangs around Konstantin. He looks very different in livery." She started examining his arms.

"Not one of the three we followed?"

"No, the ones we discounted as hangers on."

"That might have been a mistake."

"Aha!"

"What is it?"

"This." Beth held up the dead man's arm and pointed to a tattoo on his forearm. It was quite small.

"It's a hammer," Alain said.

"Yes, Konstantin has one just like it."

Back at the bar she resumed her duties. People drifted in and took tables as close to where she danced as they could. Ivan had arranged the tables in the bar to get as many in as possible which meant there was little room between them. Consequently, Mila had to put up with being groped and her bottom pinched.

She was firmly removing a man's hand from her arse when Konstantin came in with his three friends. They were followed by two more, the men from the market.

Things are warming up. Beth went to their table immediately after they sat down.

"Good evening, gentlemen, what can I get you?"

"Vodka. Bring the bottle," the man identified as being from Moscow said.

She smiled at Konstantin and blew him a kiss. He looked awkward and the others gave her flat unfriendly looks. She worried about that as she went to get their order from the bar.

Konstantin had followed her and she turned to find him in front of her.

"They will not let me take you with me."

"Not let you? I thought you were in charge?"

"It's not that simple, the group is run by a committee. I am the chairman, but they have a say in everything we do and all decisions have to be put to the vote."

"And they voted not to let you take me?"

"Yes."

"That's a strange way to run things. A leader is a leader."

"It's the way France was run during their revolution."

Ivan put a bottle of vodka on the bar with a thump followed by six glasses. Mila turned, a tear in her eye and picked them up. She turned back to Konstantin who looked wretched and gave him her best proud look. The tear ran down her cheek giving the lie to her pose.

"You are not the man I thought you to be." She pushed past him and deposited the bottle and glasses loudly on the table.

Dimitri had been supplemented by a fiddler and a drummer. The trio were quite good and were setting up when Mila asked them to play 'Volga Mat' Rodnaya', a folk song that tells that Razin, who is a captain, captures a Persian princess and spends one night with her. His men accuse him of weakness and that he has become a 'woman' in the morning. In answer to them, he throws the princess into the water and goes on a drunken binge with his men. The symbology of the dance and song were not lost on Konstantin or his friends.

Mila's second dance was to 'Lyubo, bratsy, lyubo'. A song about a Cossack army leading forty thousand men to a battle at the Terek River after which the riverbank was covered in dead men and horses. The fatally wounded hero remembers his wife, his mother, and his steed and mourns his fate. That wasn't lost on Konstantin or any of the others either.

She ignored their table from then on, leaving it to another of the girls. She strutted more than usual and let herself be pulled onto laps as she took orders. All of this kept Konstantin and his friend's attention on her and allowed several agents to sit close by and listen into their conversation.

After the bar closed and everyone had left, she was helping clear up when Konstantin came through the door. He was drunk.

"Mila, I need to talk to you."

"You said all you had to."

"That was the committee, not me!"

"I thought you were a strong man. You turn out to be weak." Her fists clenched in anger, tears ran down her cheeks.

"I am strong, I will take you with me despite what they say."

"I don't believe you. When you sober up you will do just what they tell you." Scorn dripped from every syllable.

"No, I won't." He stood as erect as his drunkenness allowed.

"Come and tell me that in the morning."

She walked away, leaving him swaying as if in a strong breeze.

The next morning Konstantin didn't show up. Nor did he show up at lunchtime. Mila was worried she had overplayed her hand, but then mid-afternoon he walked in the door. He was dressed nicely and clean. He walked directly over to Ivan and talked to him. Ivan looked cross and argued. Konstantin leaned in close and said something that made Ivan blanche then nod. Coins were passed over and Konstantin walked over to Mila.

"Have your things ready to leave in the morning," he said, then held her face in his hands and kissed her on the lips. "I always keep my word."

The door opened again and the two men from the market came in and took a table by the door.

"They will see you are safe until then." Konstantin then left.

"Safe? What do I need to be kept safe from?" she called as the door closed behind him.

There were two men on duty outside the bar all night so Beth left a coded note in the dead drop behind the beam above the table where Alain sat. It was only to be used in emergencies and she figured this counted. The next morning, she was ready at dawn and was met in the bar room by Ivan who gave her a heavy woollen coat and a hat.

"Come back safely. Don't let that idiot get you killed,"

"What did he say to you?"

"He said if I didn't let you go, he and his men would burn the bar to the ground."

The two men were waiting outside and led her across town to a warehouse. Inside were around fifty men and five large, covered waggons. She saw Konstantin and walked over to him.

"You will ride with me on the first waggon. You will stay in sight of me or my men at all times. Is that clear?"

"Yes, but why?"

"It is the price you pay for coming with us."

Ten men got into the back of the waggon and the canvas doors at the back tied shut. Konstantin got into the driver's seat and Mila got up beside him. He pulled a blanket over their laps and signalled to men by the doors. They left the warehouse just as a light fall of snow began.

Mila kept her eyes open as they turned into the road and spotted a man on a rooftop watching them. Hoping he was one of the prince's, she signed 'fifty men'. If he wasn't the sign would not mean anything.

"How far is it?"

"Schlisselburg is about thirty miles, we should get there before dark."

"Tomorrow isn't the twenty-third."

"We need a few days to prepare. The rest of the men will gather there over the next few days and weapons will be distributed."

"Is it really a fortress?"

"It was, it's been a prison for quite some time now."

"My father is held there," a man said from behind them. Mila turned and recognised him as a customer.

"Are all the men in your little army from St Petersburg?"

"About half, the rest are from Moscow, Minsk, places like that."

About one hundred men then.

"It is enough," Konstantin said. "The fortress only has thirty guards."

Schlisselburg was on the bank of Lake Ladoga at the head of the river Neva. The fortress was on Orekhovy island at the confluence of the lake and river.

Mila and Konstantin stood on the shore and looked across at the island.

"You never said it was on an island," Mila said. "It must be half a mile offshore."

"It is and that is what made it such a vital fortress in the past. It secured the frontier between Russia and Sweden."

"Well, if it is so strong, how are you going to take it?"

"In those days they had cannons to keep people out. Now they focus all their efforts on keeping people in."

"I still don't understand."

"We will get the men across at night using fishing boats. We will carry over enough explosives to destroy the gate and once we are inside will outnumber the guards."

"Just like that?"

"Yes, just like that."

It took two days to assemble the men, Mila counted one hundred and fifteen, mainly untrained. Some, only teenagers. There were a few men who had been in the army and knew something of combat. It was one of these that was put in charge of the demolition of the gate.

The powder was stored in a waggon covered by a tarpaulin. Beth snuck out of bed and made her way to it. She lifted a corner. The powder was stored in kegs that were about thirteen inches tall by eleven in diameter which told her this was probably musket powder as blasting powder came in bigger kegs. A large coil of fuse was laying on the waggon bed along with a jar of lamp oil.

It was just after midnight on the twenty-third. The raiding party assembled on the dock. A half dozen fishing boats stood ready to carry them to the island. Mila had been told to stay behind so she just stood and watched the chaos unfold.

The former soldiers were acting as sergeants and trying to get their squads into some kind of order so they could be loaded onto the boats. The plan was to get half of the men over to form a bridgehead then get the powder across and as that was being laid get the rest of the men over.

She watched as they boarded, some pushing and shoving in their excitement. The boats left. Konstantin was in the first with the rest of the committee. Mila waved goodbye. Twenty minutes later the first boat returned, and the powder kegs were loaded into it.

Beth checked her watch, there was no need to keep up the pretence any longer with the committee on the island. She walked to a shed and entered. Inside was a shuttered, reflector, signal lamp, flint, steel and tinder along with a long knife and a pair of pistols. She armed herself, tied her skirt hem up out of the way, lit the lamp and tied a white cloth around her right bicep. She stepped outside, pointed the lamp at the castle and opened and closed the shutter in a deliberate sequence. There was a single answering flash high up from one of the towers.

She checked her watch again. The boat with the powder had left and the rest of the men were boarding the boats.

Five, four, three, two, one, she looked out towards the water. There was a flash, that turned into a fireball followed by the sound of the explosion as the powder exploded. She estimated that the boat must have been close to the shore. The timer she had planted the night before had ignited the charge pretty much as she planned. The flash illuminated the boats carrying the second wave fifty yards offshore.

Suddenly there was the sound of horses and Beth pulled her pistols. Forty Cossacks formed a cordon around the dock. She walked over and found Alain with them. He had Polina, saddled and bridled on a lead rein. She mounted.

"Are you well?" he asked.

"I'm fine. It's all gone to plan so far."

"There is a company of infantry reinforcing the island."

Beth looked out across the lake. The fishing boats were still illuminated by the burning wreck of the powder boat. They had turned around and were coming back to shore. The sound of shooting drifted across from the island and she could see torches moving along the shore.

Konstantin stepped ashore from the boat. The island was quiet, the only illumination came from the lamps that burned beside the gate. He was full of nervous energy and fiddled with his musket. It didn't take long for the rest of the men of the first wave to get ashore and spread out in an arc to create the bridgehead.

The wait for the powder boat was interminable, he needed a pee, and his guts were churning. There was no sign that anyone in the fortress knew they were there. He started as he caught a single flash of a lantern on the nearest tower. He was about to mention it to the man next to him when there was a huge explosion from behind them.

"Oh my god the powder has exploded." He shouted but no one was listening. The blast deafened them and they were buffeted by the shock wave.

The gates opened and a column of men marched out. They were disciplined and formed a line. Every fifth man carried a torch. Panic spread through the rebels. Konstantin's guts turned to water and ran down his legs. He raised his musket and with shaking hands aimed at the soldiers. He fired but the shot went high.

The line presented arms. Shouts of "Don't shoot, we surrender!" came up from the men around him. The soldiers ignored them. The last thing Konstantin saw in this life was the flash of the rifles firing in volley before three balls tore his chest to shreds.

Back on the dock the fishing boats returned and some of the men scrambled ashore before realising they were surrounded by a cordon of mounted Cossacks.

"Get out of the boats," the officer ordered.

The men, frightened and confused by the turn of events, came ashore.

"You as well," he ordered the crews.

The Cossacks moved their horses to surround the men.

"I think it's time we left," Alain said, as the Cossacks drew their sabres.

London

Beth woke, stretched, and sat up. She looked to her right and smiled as Sebastian muttered something in his sleep. On her return from her mission, she had decided that she would rather lose her virginity to the man she loved than coldly on another mission as an act of duty. In any case she would be marrying him as soon as she could get her parents' permission. He had already asked her and she had accepted with all her heart.

Her mother had told her about sex, explaining things in embarrassingly graphic detail, but she had been unprepared for the sheer joy and pleasure of making love to Sebastian. He was a kind, considerate lover, who took care that she enjoyed the experience even more than he did.

She slid out of bed and padded naked across the room. She had to report to Admiral Turner to debrief after the mission in Russia.

"You look absolutely beautiful," Sebastian said.

She looked at him over her shoulder and smiled.

"I must go."

"Mustn't keep the admiral waiting."

"It's just a debrief."

"Nevertheless."

She dressed and asked a servant to summon her a Hansom Cab. It was raining, again. Admiral Turner's office was in the Foreign Office and she arrived with ten minutes to spare.

"Admiral Turner is expecting you," the non-descript clerk at the reception desk said. "Go straight up."

She went up to the third floor and knocked on an unmarked door. It was opened by a burly individual who patted her down before letting her proceed. She voluntarily gave up her dagger and pistol. But kept the weapons and tools hidden in her hair. If he couldn't find them, that was his problem.

James Turner sat behind his desk and watched her enter. She moved with the grace of a dancer, looked the image of her mother and was as ruthless as her father. She smiled at him but forewent giving him a hug.

"Hello, Chaton."

He's being formal.

"Admiral," she said carefully.

"I've read the reports on the activities in Russia. It looks like it was a job well done."

Faint praise.

"Catarina was a member of the extremist group?"

"Yes, if we had known about it before we would have found a tattoo of a hammer on her forearm. She was a committee member and was giving them information on the goings-on in the security service. The committee were all killed according to Prince Victor."

"Yes, the Russians have a record of eliminating threats, I doubt if any of the men who took part in the attempted raid survived."

Beth said nothing. She remembered the screams as the Cossacks did their work.

"Now onto your next mission."

"Aah, Admiral. Is this still part of my qualification from the academy?"

"Oh, I absolutely forgot about that. You have passed out and are now officially a junior agent." He jumped to his feet, came around the table, pulled her to her feet and hugged her. "Congratulations." He kissed her on the cheek. Then he went back behind his desk and was all business again.

"You will have two weeks to yourself then, on the 16th, you will go to Tomlins for a briefing."

"Tomlins?"

"It's a house in Kent. You will meet two agents there who have been working a case in Liverpool.

They will brief you. Now run along and enjoy your holiday."

Dismissed and none the wiser as to what her next job would be, she left. Sebastian was on duty, so she decided to go shopping. She browsed through several dress shops but nothing caught her interest, then she walked into Berkley Square and there was Manton's the gunsmith. She strolled to the door which was opened by a young man in a suit.

"How can we help you, Miss?" he said.

"What do you have in pistols that are lightweight and a repeater?"

"All we have is a two-barrelled muff pistol of .37 calibre."

"Too slow to reload. I have a Pauly that reloads fast but is only a single shot. I was hoping you might have a revolver."

"No, Miss, we are not experimenting with revolvers. Mr Manton has decided to concentrate on sporting rifles"

She left disappointed and wandered the shops aimlessly until she came upon the one her father bought his 'tools' at. She stepped inside and was recognised immediately.

"Miss Bethany," the man pronounced it Beffany being from South London. "What can I do for you today?"

"I am looking for personal protection weapons that are easily concealed." She improvised on the spot.

"Naa then, I might just 'ave the fing."

God, you can cut that accent with a knife.

He went out the back and returned with a pair of small, double-barrelled pistols

"What do you fink of them then?"

"80 bore, percussion fired, small enough to be hidden anywhere," she assessed.

"Made in America by Lill of Louth"

She examined one, it was a turning-barrel design where you fired the top one, then turned the barrels to bring the bottom one into line. It had percussion nipples on both barrels, and you would have to be careful you didn't knock the bottom one off when turning the barrels. While it was being carried the lower cap was protected by a brass plate. It had Lill engraved on one side of the action and Louth on the other.

"Interesting. How much?"

"Eight quid the pair."

That was a lot of money, she guessed that in America they would sell for twenty or thirty dollars a pair and she doubted he paid that much.

"I'll give you five."

"Er now, Miss, you be robbing me at that. How about you gives me seven?"

She knew where this would end. "I will go to six and you can throw in that pair of punch daggers," she said, indicating a nasty pair of knives with T bar grips.

"Done," the shop owner said.

As he packaged the pieces up, he said, "Could I interest you in a set of the latest lock picks? Even your esteemed father ain't got these yet." He produced a leather wallet which he opened to show a range of steel picks that looked like they could open any lock."

"How much for them?"

"For you, Miss, ten bob."

That was also a lot of money but as far as she knew no one else sold that type of merchandise in London.

"That's a shilling a pick."

"But think what you could make out of them."

She laughed, then abruptly sobered and said, "If anyone else said that I would shoot him."

The shop owner gulped and said, "Now, Miss, you don't want to do anyfing rash to old Bill."

Beth took the wallet from his fingers and put it in her purse from which she took a pouch that jingled. She opened it and counted out six guineas and one and a half crowns.

"I want a second set for my beau. You can keep the tanner as a tip." She grinned as she opened the door.

When Sebastian came home after his watch ended, he couldn't find Beth anywhere so asked a servant where she was.

"In the cellar, Sir, practising with her guns."

He went down and carefully stuck his head around the corner. There was Beth practising with a pair of guns he hadn't seen before.

"New toys?" he said and ducked back. Just in case.

"I heard you coming," she said, even though she had bound a cloth around her ears to protect them from the retort as she fired.

"I thought it wouldn't be a good idea to surprise you."

"True, it could get you shot," she said and sidled up to him. She slipped her arms around his neck and kissed him, then pressed the wallet of picks into his hand.

When they broke apart he opened the wallet.

"I got you a set when I bought mine from old Bill. They are the latest." He kissed her in thanks then picked up one of the guns.

"Nasty little beast. Hit someone in the chest with that and it will stop them cold."

She indicated a manikin stood some ten feet away. He checked the cap and shot from the hip. The bullet flew wide and splatted into the wall behind it. He turned the barrel and fired again this time the bullet hit the white patch over where the heart would be.

"Pulls right," he said.

"I know, that was why I was practising."

"Any news?" he said and put the gun on the table with its brother.

"We have two weeks before I have to go to Kent."

The highlight of her holiday was a ball thrown by the guards at Horse Guards. A glittery affair with the regimental band providing the music. Officers from lieutenant upwards were present with their wives or girlfriends and were waited on by ensigns.

Sebastian was in full mess dress uniform. Rifles green doe-skin jacket, embellished with black Russian braid chevrons, red embroidered cuffs, high collar, and bowtie. Embroidered waistcoat of the same material. White silk shirt. Black mess trousers (overalls) with two-inch black worsted-wool-braid band down the seam. Soft leather, Wellington boots.

Beth chose a deep emerald-green, silk ball gown with a fitted bodice. It was off the shoulder with a square neckline and puffs around her upper arms. It was embroidered with vines that ran down from the neckline to the hem either side of the centre line. She had woven a strand of pearls with an emerald drop that hung in the centre of her forehead, through her intricately arranged hair. Around her neck glittered a diamond and emerald necklace. Long silk gloves covered her arms to her elbows and bracelets that matched her necklace adorned her wrists.

Everyone knew they were inseparable but that didn't stop the senior officers asking her to dance. They had a marvellous time and didn't get home to the Stockley house in Grosvenor Square, until the early hours of the morning.

The next morning Sebastian had duty at the palace at eight o'clock which meant he had only a couple of hours sleep. Beth slept in, had a late breakfast then went down to the stables. Polina and Melody vied for her attention, and she treated them both with carrots. The two horses generally got along but were kept in separate stalls as Polina had a tendency to bite if not given her own space.

She chose Polina for her daily ride and saddled her. Polina wasn't trained for a side saddle, so she fitted her with the

Russian-style saddle and bridle she had gotten for her in St Petersburg. It was a very comfortable rig and fitted the horse perfectly.

She rode to Hyde Park and set her to a trot. The park wasn't very busy and soon she found an open track where she could canter. Hyde Park was considered a safe place in general, mainly because it was usually busy but for some reason it was very thinly populated that morning. She stayed alert as she entered the wooded area in the centre of the park.

Something felt wrong, the birds had stopped singing. She slowed to a walk, holding the reins in her left hand, her right in the pocket of her riding habit. Then a ray of sun came through the leaves of the branches and illuminated a rope strung across the path ahead of her. She prepared to kick Polina into a canter as she turned her around, but a man surged out of the bushes and grabbed her bridle. Another came at her from the side.

Beth's awareness expanded and time seemed to slow, she dropped the reins as her right hand pulled out one of her new pistols. She shot the man coming from the side as he reached up to pull her from the horse. The bullet hit the bridge of his nose and ruined his face. She felt Polina kick backwards and heard a scream. She turned the barrels to bring the loaded one into line. Polina seemed to have had some training as a war horse as she bit the man holding her bridle and when he let go reared and kicked him in the head. Beth grabbed the reins and turned her a full circle.

Behind them was a man lying on the ground, clutching his knee. It looked shattered and there was a fair amount of blood. A nasty-looking club lay on the ground beside him. The man she shot lay still, unconscious, or dead she couldn't say. The man who Polina had kicked in the head lay on the ground with blood coming from his eyes and ears.

She became aware of whistles. A police constable was running down the track towards her. She lowered the hammer on her pistol and put it in her pocket. The newly promoted Sergeant Quigley slowed to a stop, looked at the scattered bodies, then at Beth.

"Are you alright, Miss Bethany?"

"I am fine, no thanks to these idiots," she said. "They tried to pull me from my horse."

Quigley eyed Polina cautiously. Her eyes still showed the whites, her nostrils flared and her ears back. Beth dismounted and patted her neck.

"She was amazing, she took down those two before I could."

More constables arrived and one left to fetch an inspector. Polina snorted and pawed the ground.

"Steady, girl," Beth said softly, and rubbed her nose, "it's all over now."

Her calmness, the caresses and soft voice soothed the horse, and she calmed down. Beth dropped the reins on the ground and walked away from her.

"Will she stay there?" Quigley asked.

"She is Cossack trained, if I drop her reins she stays put, if I just leave them on her neck, she will follow me wherever I go."

"Cossack? That's them Russian's innit?" he said and bent to examine the unconscious man.

"Yes. Is he dead?"

"He ain't good. We need to get him to a doctor. We have one at the station we can call in, but I think your horse stove in his skull."

A horse-drawn police van arrived, and a man in a suit and bowler hat got down from where he was sat next to the driver.

"This is a fine mess," he said, eyeing up the scene. He spotted the rope. "Tried to unhorse you, Miss?"

"Yes, but I spotted it in time to avoid it. Then that man grabbed my bridle and that one tried to pull me off my horse."

"What about him?"

"He came up behind me and got kicked in the knee."

"By your horse?"

"She's a Cossack-trained horse, Sir," Quigley said as if he knew that all along.

"Is she now, and what is a Cossack-trained horse doing in Hyde Park?"

Beth bit off the sarcastic answer she had on the tip of her tongue and said, "I recently bought her in St Petersburg, I didn't know she was war trained until now. Who are you?"

The inspector made notes and when he finished looked at her and said, "Inspector John Stone and who are you, Miss?"

"Bethany Stockley."

"You have a gun?"

"Two actually," she said and took out the pair and handed them over. "Careful, they are loaded."

"Now what is a young lass like you doing with these?"

"Can I have a word, Inspector?" Quigley said.

He took Stone to one side and said something to him. Stone glanced at Beth several times. Then walked back to her.

"The Right Honourable Bethany Stockley, daughter of Viscount Stockley?"

"Yes," she said. "Are you new to this area?"

He ignored that and said, "You will have to come with us to the police house. I need a statement."

"Am I being charged?"

"Not at the moment."

At that time Sir Robert Peel hadn't formalised the police force in London and what passed for a police force was volunteer in the main. However, because of the wealth of that part of London it had a police force funded by donations form the residents. The Police House was in Park Street.

Beth made a statement and signed it. A magistrate was called and oversaw the investigation. The injured men were treated by a local doctor and the dead man taken to the mortuary. The inspector and magistrate had a long conversation.

"Miss Bethany Stockley, I am charging you with the manslaughter of Cedric Sands," he said. "You will be held here to await a hearing."

"May I send some messages?"

"You may."

Beth wrote a note to Turner and another to their family solicitor Mr Mullins.

Mullins arrived first and asked Beth what had happened. She told him the facts. He got up and went straight to the magistrate. Voices were raised and it was turning into an outright row when the door opened, and James Turner walked in with a serious-looking man dressed in a cloak and top hat.

"Gentlemen," Turner said and both Mullins and the magistrate shut up and looked at him. "I am Admiral James Turner and this is Sir Robert Barker the Chief Metropolitan Police Magistrate for London. I believe you have arrested my goddaughter Lady Stockley for manslaughter?"

Beth heard the use of the honorific and smiled. It wasn't her title, but James was using it for effect.

"It's a clear case of self-defence," Mullins said.

"What is a nineteen-year-old doing carrying these?" the inspector said holding up the pistols. "She shot a man in the face!"

Sir Robert held up his hands, "Gentlemen please, let me see her statement and the police notes." He sat at the desk and read slowly. He looked across to where Beth was sitting. "Shot through the bridge of the nose?"

"He was only three feet away, I could hardly miss."

"Have you charged the horse?" he asked the magistrate.

"What? Why would I charge a horse?"

"Well it seems it assaulted two of the men and on the basis of your charge sheet it would seem it is as equally culpable as Lady Bethany."

At that point the doctor entered. "Killed one, he just passed."

"This is, as Mr Mullins has said, a clear case of self-defence. Not a jury in England would find either Lady Bethany or her horse guilty of manslaughter."

"But the guns."

"Are for her self-defence. She is the daughter of a wealthy man and not only my goddaughter but the king's as well," James Turner said.

The magistrate and inspector gave in and Beth was released. Once outside she stood by Polina after hugging James. They could still hear the argument going on inside. It seemed to revolve around ladies of quality carrying guns.

Sir Robert came out of the building, shook James's hand, and stepped over to Bethany. He handed her the guns.

"Thought you would want these back."

"I didn't like to ask for them, they were so angry."

"You offended their sensibilities, which is no reason to charge you. This is your horse?"

"Yes, Polina."

Polina's ears went up at the sound of her name.

Sir Robert looked her over and nodded to her right foreleg. "You need to get that piece of scalp off." He bowed and went to his carriage.

"Well, that went well," Beth said.

"I will recommend that the inspector be replaced. He is bigoted. Let me see those guns."

She handed one over. He weighed it in his hand. "Nice balance, where did you get them?"

"Hunter's."

"The shop in Shackle Lane?"

"Yes, that's the one."

He handed it back. "Be careful, this city isn't safe."

"That's why I—"

"Carry the guns, I know. You could also take an escort. Your father employs several experienced men."

Beth wanted to kick back against that but wisely held her peace.

"Now off home with you, Sebastian will finish his duty in an hour."

He walked away. Beth gave his back a look and as he got to the corner, he looked back and grinned.

Kent

Beth's carriage turned into a long, impressive drive through parkland. The coach was one of the service's and she wasn't told her destination, only that she would be there for three days. She had also been instructed to bring her 'tools' by which they meant all the things she might need for a possible mission. The coach passed through a large formal garden with a walled garden in the distance. It was all very pretty in the late spring sunshine.

The coach crossed a wooden bridge over what looked like a dry moat, through a tunnel, turned and pulled to a stop inside what was evidently a large fort. *Near the sea. I can smell it. Deal? Walmer?* she thought as she climbed out of the coach and looked around at the imposing walls and saw that the tunnel had been through a gatehouse built into a round bastion. *Round bastions and a round keep. Only three places like that, Walmer, Sandown and Deal and I bet this is Walmer.*

A man came out of the door to the keep and walked towards her. He was followed but a pair of footmen in livery who started to unload her baggage.

"Chaton. Welcome to Walmer Castle. My name is Charles Handy, secretary to the Earl of Liverpool. Please come with me. The men will take care of your things."

She glanced at the footmen who had her bags in hand and waited to follow her inside. She noted that they both had lumps under their coats at waist level.

Handy gently took her arm and led her into the keep. Just inside the doors, on the left, was a room where four men sat relaxing. All wore guns. Beyond that they started up a staircase to the first floor and a long corridor. The walls were decorated more like a residence than a fortress with pictures of past residents.

They entered a rather well-appointed bedroom with a view over the gardens.

"This is your room for your stay with us. You can freshen up after your long trip and I will come and get you in an hour." Her bags were left beside the large bed. She opened one and took out her clothes and hung them in the wardrobe or put them in drawers as required. Her one-piece black coverall was put in a drawer with her chamois-soled slippers and equipment belt.

The second bag was heavier than the first and held a variety of weapons, tools, and her forging kit. These she also stored away in drawers according to what they were.

She poured water from the jug on the wash stand into the bowl and washed her face and hands. She examined herself in the mirror, *acceptable.*

She was reading a copy of today's *Times* when Handy knocked on her door. He led her down the corridor, up another set of stairs and along another corridor. He knocked on a door and entered before there was an answer.

Turner, Canning, another older man and two younger men sat around a table. They all stood as she entered.

"Gentlemen," she said, nodding in greeting and took the offered chair. The older man was expensively dressed with a diamond-capped pin holding his neck cloth in place. His suit was conservative in style, hair greying at the temples, hands uncalloused, fingernails trimmed and polished. *A merchant or banker, maybe a diplomat.* The other two were in their thirties, wore nondescript clothing, no jewellery and kept their hands folded in front of them. *Agents.*

"We are here at the home of the Prime Minister as the security here is absolute. Whatever is spoken of in this room must not be divulged to anyone. Is that clear?"

Everyone nodded.

"Mr Rush is the American Ambassador and has made a request on behalf of his government. Sir, would you kindly fill us in on the situation and how we can help."

"As you all know we have recently purchased Florida from the Spanish and on top of that Spain has lost control of many of its South American holdings. The consequences of that are they no longer control or constrain the actions of privateers in their former territories and we have seen an increase in piracy against shipping in the Gulf of Mexico and along the south and east coasts of America. From what our agents in the south have found, letters of marque were issued, intended for the privateers to attack Spanish shipping, but they have become increasingly indiscriminate about who or where they strike."

Turner took over. "The Royal Navy is patrolling the Caribbean and has had some success in limiting the piratical activities there, but it seems someone is feeding information to the privateers about ship movements and some of that information is coming from Britain."

"Excuse me, Sir, but wouldn't any information of when ships are sailing be out of date by the time it got from here to the Caribbean?" Beth said.

"Now there's the nub of the thing, they are somehow getting information on when ships are due to leave, far enough in advance to set up an intercept."

"What ships are they using?" Beth asked.

"There are a few with former Spanish war ships or converted merchantmen but the majority are in schooner-sized ships. Why do you ask?"

"Just interested, as my father has experience of pirates in that region."

"We think that there is a shipping broker in Liverpool that is the main source of information," one of the agents said.

"Hound and Felix have been investigating this for us for the last months and have traced the information to a broker," Turner said. "What we want you to do is use your specialist skills to find evidence and plant information that will lead the pirates into a trap."

"Why do I need to spend three days here?"

"They will brief you on what they have found so far and you can refresh your breaking-and-entering skills."

Beth didn't think her skills needed refreshing at all, but she said nothing. Turner must have his reasons.

The meeting was closed and she went back to her room to prepare for dinner. Turner had told her to dress appropriately for dinner with senior people. She dressed in a gown of light blue satin and arranged her hair in a Greek classical style so it flowed over one shoulder. She wore a simple gold necklace with a pendant that featured a black opal. She wondered at that as she examined herself in the mirror as the opal was blue, with green, red and ochre flecks.

A servant guided her to the dining room. She swept in with all the poise her mother had drilled into her. Even so, she was hard put to conceal her surprise at the sight of Prime Minister, Robert Jenkins, Earl of Liverpool. The men turned and Jenkins' eyes widened slightly when he saw her. He was moderately tall, dressed in black with a white shirt and neck cloth, grey hair, and a handsome face. She noticed his left eye was larger than his right and seemed to bulge slightly.

She curtsied and he stepped forward to bow over her hand

"I am told I am to refer to you as Chaton, kitten seems an appropriate name."

"Beware of her claws, Prime Minister, she has hidden weapons," Turner said, coming up beside her.

"No doubt," he leaned in close and whispered sotto voice, "I have met your mother, a woman one would not care to cross."

Beth didn't say she had seen him at the balls she had attended. He was married and it was rumoured that his wife was ill.

"How is your wife, Sir?"

"Not well at all, I am afraid. She is at our house in London. I will return there tomorrow."

Dinner was a delicious four-course affair with wine. Beth only took a single glass and sipped it, preferring water. After dinner she left the men to smoke cigars and drink brandy. She had an early start in the morning.

The morning came and she dressed for a run. Loose trousers, a white blouse and soft-soled shoes. She let herself out and set off. She planned to circumnavigate the grounds, a run of about three miles, then arms practice with Hound and Felix. She set her pace to what her father called a wolf lope. It was cool, being late spring, and it took a while to warm up. She saw a few estate workers who gawped at the sight of a woman dressed in trousers running around the track that defined the perimeter. She didn't see the ambassador stood in the window of his room watching her with a telescope.

She returned to the castle and found her two colleagues waiting in the courtyard. A thick woven rush mat covered by canvas was laid out as a training surface. She stretched and performed a few ballet moves. Felix stepped onto the mat carrying a six-foot-long staff. Beth looked to Hound just in time to catch a staff he tossed to her. She twirled it, finding its pivot point and assessing its weight.

Felix stepped in and made an attack swinging at her hip. She blocked and returned the compliment towards his head. The contest settled and the sound of the staffs striking each other echoed around the walls. A small audience gathered including some of the security team. The staff fight ended with Beth halting a strike to his head just an inch from contact.

Hound then took over and stepped onto the mat holding a wooden practice knife. Beth selected one from a table of weapons and looked at it disdainfully. She sighed and stepped back on the mat. She turned the step into a spinning attack without any warning at all. Hound did well to avoid contact. He had heard of her skills from his friend Bomber at the academy and knew she would be a handful. He was an accomplished knife fighter and had to be at his best to defend against the sustained attack.

Beth stepped back, breaking off contact and saluted him. He had fended off all of her attacks. He took the initiative and launched his own. She defended skilfully, she was very fast and light on her feet. He felt her hesitate, just for a fraction of a second and probed again. Yes, she was definitely a fraction slower there. He feigned an attack to her other side then switched to the vulnerable area. She wasn't there. He froze as her knife was laid across his throat from behind.

"Got you."

There was applause from the audience.

She was allowed a ten-minute break then Hound stepped forward.

"Let's see how good you are in unarmed combat."

This set off a series of bets between members of the audience and out of the corner of her eye she saw Turner and the ambassador watching from a balcony.

He took his stance and Beth recognised it as one Chin used. This was going to be interesting. He bounced on the balls of his feet. For a big man he looked very mobile. She took a defensive stance and made ready.

He threw a punch which she dodged. It was only a tester. He was seeing how fast she was and how her stamina was holding out. She spun and tried a kick to his head; he ducked under it and used his forearm to push her ankle around increasing her spin speed. She went with it and pirouetted. He anticipated that and swept her standing leg from under her. She rolled away and came to her feet.

He was on her in a second using his weight to knock her back to the ground. He had her in a choke hold, his legs wrapped around her. It was a sleeper hold and restricted the blood supply to her brain. She dug her nails into his arm in an attempt to loosen his grip. He just grunted and squeezed harder. She had no choice; she tapped his arm in submission.

They took their stances again. Beth wiped the sweat from her eyes and focussed. She had to keep him at a distance, he was bigger and stronger than her. Her long legs were her main advantage. She threw a straight kick towards his head forcing him back. He circled looking for an opening then tried to step inside her guard. She grabbed his shirt with both hands and rolled backwards, planted her foot in his stomach and threw him. He rolled off his shoulder and came to his feet.

She faced him, he shifted to a wrestler's stance. She wasn't going to let him do that, she changed to a side on stance and held her hands up like a boxer while bouncing on the balls of her feet. She raised her foot and threatened a kick. He went defensive. She retracted it and circled looking for an opening. He followed her, moving his upper body to make himself a harder target. She probed, he responded, he attacked, she retreated.

Suddenly with a shout she stepped forward jabbing at his face, he blocked and grabbed her arm. She stepped into his body, twisting. He braced for a throw. Something hit him in the back of the head. The lights went out.

He came to and found her bent over him. She looked into her eyes, grey/green, he wasn't sure.

"Are you alright?"

"I'll live. What did you do?"

"Kicked you."

"How?"

"Stand up, I will show you."

They stood and she moved into the position they had ended in. Her right leg came up behind her and the heel of her foot touched the lump on the back of his head.

"The ballet moves," he sighed.

They cooled down and went to dress for breakfast. Jenkins had already left for London; he was concerned for his wife. At breakfast they were joined by Turner and the ambassador.

"Good morning. That was quite a show."

"Good morning, Mr Rush."

"Call me Dick. You cost me a guinea."

"You bet on Hound?"

"I did. You surprised us all with that kick."

"It was a move my mother taught me."

"Really? I would like to meet her!"

"You may have already without knowing it," Turner said.

"I have? Where?"

Turner just smiled at him then winked at Beth.

After breakfast, Dick left for London leaving the agents to share their knowledge.

"We found that many of the ships that were captured had come from Liverpool and were on the return leg of their trips. That got us to thinking that maybe someone is letting them know when these ships leave Liverpool or at least when they plan to leave," Hound said.

"What we thought was happening was that someone was giving the monthly shipping schedule to someone on a ship bound for Cartagena or somewhere like that. So we started looking at the shipping lists and crews, especially fast ships that left at the beginning of the month," Felix said.

"I see," Beth said, "they take six weeks or so to get across but that doesn't matter because they get there and can work out when the slower ships should arrive and then know roughly what time they will leave."

Felix looked at her for a few seconds working out what she just said. "I think you have it."

Beth treated him to a vacant, beaming, smile. He wasn't fooled.

"We then found out who the agents were for those ships and guess what? They all used the same one," Felix continued.

"We specialise in investigative work, so we asked for an agent who is a specialist in infiltration and breaking and entering. They gave us you," Hound said, sounding unconvinced.

They asked Beth to demonstrate her breaking-and-entering skills. She said she would do so by leaving the castle after dinner then breaking back in and purloining items from each of their rooms. They in turn would make it as difficult as possible by alerting the guards and setting traps.

Beth chose the wee small hours before dawn when the guards were coming up to the ends of their watch. Dressed in her black one piece she approached the castle. As a matter of routine, she had studied it for blind spots and weak points.

Approaching from the east through the gardens, Beth easily avoided the sentries on patrol. Dropping quietly down into the dry moat she chose a spot between the north and east bastions for her entry point as it was in the moon's shadow. She stopped for a moment and gathered herself, doing what Chin would call, focussing her chi. She placed her hands on the wall and felt for bumps and crevasses. Finding holds to her liking, she proceeded to climb and slipped up the wall like a spider.

At the top she paused before climbing over the parapet, listening for footsteps. A guard walked by, his boots clicking on the stones. She waited until he passed, then slipped onto the gun platform and padded across to a window. She sprung the catch with a slim jim and cracked it open enough to slip the quill of a goose feather along the opening. She smiled as she felt it touch something.

They trapped the windows. She checked the wall at the end then stepped back a few paces and ran at it. She turned that momentum into upward movement and reached a waterspout which she grabbed. She heard footsteps again and froze. The guard passed her and disappeared around the corner. Beth heaved and lifted herself up until she could get a leg up and onto the roof.

She lay breathing heavily on the sloping roof until she recovered then moved up to a skylight she had seen earlier. A little bit of fiddling undid the bolt, and she lifted it after checking for traps. She propped it open and lowered her head down until she could see the corridor below. It was empty. Gripping the edge, she performed a forward roll that ended with her dropping silently to the floor.

She paused and examined her surroundings, using her peripheral vision which was a thousand times more receptive to the low light to scan for traps and spotted a trip wire. Using the quill, she moved along the corridor checking for more trip wires at both ground level and up to three feet above the floor.

She came to Felix's bedroom door. Employing an instrument used by doctors and midwives to listen to babies' hearts, she checked the door. She could hear snoring from inside. She checked the doorknob. There was no lock, but she had to assume the door was trapped. She carefully turned the knob; it was relatively new and moved easily but she didn't rush. There was no sense of resistance, so she opened the door a crack and slipped a U-shaped quill through the gap to check for anything attached to the door. Careful not to push the door open any further she ran the quill around the frame as far as she could. Finding nothing, she edged it open a little further. This time she could test further along the top edge and discovered something. There was enough moonlight coming through the un-curtained window for her to slip a mirror mounted on a thin rod through. There was a piece of string. Where it went she couldn't tell but it was attached to a nail in the top of the door.

She went to a pouch on her belt and took out a strange-looking device. It had a clamp at one end, tightened by a screw, with what looked like a pair of forceps on an articulated arm attached to it.

She clamped the device to the door frame then gently opened the door enough to get the articulated arm and forceps through. She locked them on the string. Happy it was secured she cut the string at the nail. Now she could open the door fully.

Moving as quiet as the cat she was named after, she moved across the room and looked down at the sleeping agent then checked the thread and saw it was attached to a sprung-loaded bell. A piece of cloth stuffed under the clapper sorted that out.

She looked at his wash table and picked up a leather case. It held a vanity set. She pocketed it then opened another pouch on her belt and removed something which she lay on the pillow beside his head.

Beth left the room as quietly as she had entered. She recovered the clamp, closed, and relocked the door before moving on to Hound's room. Repeating the process she followed before, she heard him snoring and found the door was unlocked. She cracked it and felt resistance. She took a bottle of light oil from a pouch and, using the built in pipette, treated the hinges. She tried again, listening for a change in Hound's breathing. It moved better so she ran through her check for traps.

Finding nothing she used the mirror to look into the room. The bed was empty, so she scanned around. Hound was sitting in a chair, asleep, his head lolling to one side. She opened the door far enough to slip through and padded across to where he was sitting. He had a pistol on his lap. She gently took it and replaced it with an object from her pouch.

The next morning, dressed in a pretty summer dress, she arrived at the gate having stayed overnight at a local inn and eaten a hearty breakfast. The guards immediately detained her and took her to the dining room where Canning, Turner, Hound and Felix were waiting. Canning and Turner looked amused while Hound and Felix looked somewhat chagrined.

"Good morning, gentlemen," Beth said brightly with a curtsy.

"Good morning, Chaton." Turner and Canning replied.

"I believe you have some items that belong to these gentlemen."

"You mean these?" Beth said and laid the vanity set and pistol on the table. "It is safe. I blew out the priming."

"Is it loaded?" Canning asked.

"With rock salt I believe," Beth answered, giving Hound a smile.

Canning frowned at Hound who looked back unapologetically.

"I hope you liked my gifts," Beth said.

"Gifts?" Turner said, raising his eyebrows in question.

Hound placed a red rose on the table. "On my lap in place of the pistol," he said.

Felix produced a second, "On my pillow."

Turner burst out laughing and Canning joined them. After a moment the two agents joined in.

"Excellent, I think Chaton has proved beyond any doubt that despite her only having recently graduated from the academy, she is well suited for the mission."

"Was there any doubt?" Beth said.

"We were concerned that such a young and inexperienced agent was suitable," Felix said.

"But you have proved yourself more than capable," Hound finished.

Liverpool

Liverpool developed rapidly as trade with the Caribbean grew and the port on the river Dee silted up. Housing and grand buildings were being constructed to make it the second city after London. Beth had a room in a modest guest house on Vernon Street. It was clean and vermin free, which was important, she vividly remembered the bed bugs in Russia and had no desire to repeat the experience.

Beth's target had an office near the docks in Old Hall Street and lived in the newly built Catherine Street. As far as her landlady was concerned, she was a governess looking for a position in the city. She wore a black dress and tied her hair up in a bun. The dress was cut to show the white linen blouse that buttoned up to the neck with a ribbon 'bow tie', the skirt flared with many petticoats. Black shoes with one and a half inch heels, and pinchbeck buckles finished the ensemble nicely.

Visiting the area where the target lived and worked was her first priority. Her governess dress distinguished her as an upper servant, and she would be pretty much overlooked by the middle classes.

Catherine Street was part of an affluent suburb that was home to many of the merchants and business owners in the city. The houses were three story plus servant's quarters in the basement, in neat terraces and could as easily have been in London as Liverpool. The roads were dimly lit with gas lights at night and watchmen patrolled. Liverpool didn't have a police force, and, with the proximity of the docks and the associated criminals, the watch was paid for by the residents. The back of the house had a garden that backed onto a path that ran between the terrace and the one it backed onto. This was mainly used by servants and was unlit. The houses had high back walls and gates that were locked.

Old Hall Street was a mixture of warehouses and commercial buildings. The office she was looking for was on the second floor of one of the commercial buildings. A ship's chandler was on the ground, and the offices of a wool merchant on the first. Access to the first and second floors was via a staircase through a door in an alley that ran up the side of the building. As she stood looking up at the building a pair of arms came around her waist.

"What 'ave we got 'ere den?" a high-pitched male voice with a thick Liverpool accent said.

She looked down at the hairy arms and an unshaven face brushed against her cheek. His breath reeked of beer.

"Let me go, you oaf," Beth said.

"Or you will do wha'? Scream?"

Beth sighed; this was wasting her time. She reached up to her bonnet and pulled out a hat pin. Six inches long and made of steel it entered his forearm and hit bone.

"Fuck!" he shouted and let her go. He stood looking at the rivulet of blood running from the hole then at Beth who stood smiling at him, pin in hand.

"Next one goes through an eye," she said, turned and walked away.

The lout pulled himself together as she turned the corner into the busy Chapple Street. By the time he got there she had disappeared.

Hound and Felix reported that Elfrid James Esq., had two children and a wife that was frail. They had overheard him saying to an associate that he would look for a governess and they thought it a golden opportunity to gain access. An advert appeared in the *Liverpool Mercury* four days after she arrived. Beth prepared an application letter and references from a previous employer, went to the address, and knocked on the door of the house. A maid answered.

"I am here concerning the position of governess that is advertised in today's *Mercury*," Beth said and handed over her application letter.

The maid looked surprised, took the letter and shut the door in her face with a, "Wait here."

She returned ten minutes later and said, "Do you have references?"

"I do."

"Come in, the mistress will see you."

She was led into the sitting room. The mistress of the house sat in an armchair with a blanket over her lap. She had a pallid complexion, looked tired, and was thin.

"Ma'am," Beth said in greeting.

"Elizabeth Burnley?"

"Yes, Ma'am."

"Your letter says you are from Sheffield."

"Yes Ma'am, I was born there." Beth found a Sheffield accent easy to imitate as her mother came from there originally and still spoke with it.

"Why have you moved to Liverpool?"

"It's a growing city, Ma'am, and cleaner than Sheffield. The ironworks, you know."

"I have heard the air reeks of smoke there."

"It does, Ma'am, and it's impossible to keep things clean."

"Your letter says you were employed as a governess there?"

"For Mr and Mrs Barlow. They had a boy, but he caught tuberculosis and died six months ago." A tear welled up in her eye at the memory.

"That was unfortunate. Do you have a reference from the Barlows?"

Beth handed over the letter. Mrs James read it, folded it, and put it on her lap.

"I have a seven-year-old boy and a six-year-old girl. They need to be tutored in manners and etiquette. They also need to be educated, the boy will be going to boarding school in the future and needs to be prepared."

Beth was ready for that and said, "I can teach maths, English, Latin and etiquette."

"What are your views on discipline?"

"Children have to know their place, have a work ethic instilled in them and learn how to behave in company. I am firm but fair."

Mrs James looked at her steadily for a long moment.

"I will let you know. I wish to interview others before I choose."

"I understand, Ma'am."

Beth treated the interview as a reconnaissance. She considered the odds of getting the position too small to put her eggs in that basket. She had noted the number of servants, the design of the windows and what type of catches were on them. But first she wanted to visit the office.

It was a dark night with only the sliver of a moon, a scudding overcast and mist rising from the river Mersey. She dressed in men's clothing, trousers, shirt, waistcoat, cap and boots. She changed the way she walked to make it more masculine and would pass for a man unless someone got very close in which case, they would either die or be unconscious in an instant.

Entering the alley beside the building she tried the door and found it locked. She took her wallet of picks from her pocket and quickly opened it. Inside it was as black as pitch and she relocked the door by feel. Creeping up the stairs to the second floor she found the door to the office. Opening it was no more a challenge than the one below. Once inside she went to the single window and drew the curtain before lighting the gas light on the wall.

The office was surprisingly opulent. A heavy desk and chair that were very well made, a plush rug on the floor, a couple of expensive club chairs with an occasional table between them. Against the wall a sideboard with a cut glass tantalus on it with expensive wine and spirit glasses. She frowned; this didn't seem to be the office of a simple shipping broker.

There was a desk for a clerk in a side office. Again, better made than you would expect. On it was a large book. She opened it and found it was the ledger where the business was recorded with the fees that were charged. It had columns for income and outgoings and according to it, Jones made a modest profit.

"That's bollocks," she said to herself. She put it down and searched the desk then the shelves on the wall. There were ledgers there for the last eight years and according to them there was no way Jones could afford the house in Catherine's Street.

The next day she met with Felix.

"If I understand you correctly, Jones' legitimate business could not sustain his lifestyle?"

"That's about it. I checked his accounting ledgers for the last eight years and there is no way he could. He has to be getting income from somewhere which isn't accounted for."

"Just selling the shipping lists would not net him enough either."

"I need to get into his house and search it for hidden records."

"How is the job application going?"

"I've heard nothing yet. Has she seen many more women?"

"Only one and she was a plant from us who I can guarantee will not be acceptable. We intercepted any others and put them off."

Beth didn't ask how they did that.

A letter was hand delivered by a servant confirming Elizabeth had been selected for the position and giving her the terms of employment. She would be living in, paid two hundred pounds a year and get Sundays off. She was asked to start at her earliest convenience.

Better pack then, she smiled to herself and put her meagre possessions in her carpet bag. She paid the landlady for an extra day in lieu of notice and walked to the house in Catherine Street. The door opened and a haggard-looking servant opened the door. The sound of screaming children came from upstairs.

"Lord, not a moment too soon," he said and ushered her in.

She did not see the lady of the house as she was shown directly to her room on the third floor. It wasn't large but had a fireplace, a clean bed and an armchair. She would eat with the children.

She put her clothes away then followed the sound of shouting and screaming to a nursery on the same floor. She opened the door to see the children running amok.

"That will be quite enough of that!" she barked in a commanding voice.

The children stopped mid-flight and looked at her.

"I am your new governess, and I will not have you disturbing the peace of this household. We shall have plenty of time for play on your daily visit to the park. You may call me Miss Beth."

The boy looked defiantly at her, so she stared him down.

"Now we will begin properly. Good morning, children."

She looked at them expectantly and was rewarded with,

"Good morning, Miss Beth."

"Excellent, now here are some ground rules which will not be broken. One, you will be polite and courteous at all times.

Two, you will keep yourselves clean and presentable at all times. Three, you will attend your lessons diligently every day. Four, you will have fun."

At the last, the children looked surprised. Beth gave them no time to dwell on it. She marched up to them and inspected behind their ears and checked their fingernails.

"Grubby in the extreme, you will bathe before I teach you."

Beth pulled the bellpull and requested a tin bath, warm water, and soap. The children looked horrified. When the bath and water had been delivered, she had them strip and get in. Both were thoroughly scrubbed until they shone, then dried and dressed in clean clothes. The air in the room was decidedly fresher afterwards.

"If you keep yourselves clean then this needn't happen more than once a week. Now I want to see how much you know."

She tested their maths and writing skills, both of which were lacking. She decided to start with maths and used slates to teach them addition and subtraction. In the afternoon she took them to the park. She ate dinner with the children after which the master of the house made himself known to her.

"So, you are the new governess. What's your name girl?"

"Elizabeth, Sir."

He looked at the children who were sitting on the floor playing quietly.

"Well, you seem to have things under control here," he said awkwardly.

"Thank you, Sir." She projected prim and proper.

"What time will they go to bed?"

"Eight o'clock, Sir."

"Good, excellent. Well good evening to you."

"Good evening."

He left.

He is not used to dealing with servants.

Beth let the household get used to her for a few days then started gradually to broaden the area of the house she was seen in. She discovered the master's study, locked, and learnt that no one was allowed in except one maid who dusted it once a week. She noted he was visited by various captains, which given his profession, wasn't unusual. Beth decided she needed to listen in on their conversations. She remembered a story her father had told about a restaurant they had set up in Paris with the sole aim of listening in on people's conversations. They had utilised the gas lamps' piping as listening tubes. She wondered if she could do the same.

Reality set in almost immediately. The pipes were far too complicated for her to modify. She thought on the problem and coming up with no answer she let it go and slept on it. The next morning, she was teaching the children when a maid came in carrying fresh linens for the beds. She was one of the chattier girls in the household.

"Lord, I had to be quick gettin' these," she said. "His lordship is 'avin a chat with one of his captains and the linen cupboard is right next door to his office. He don't like anyone hanging around when he's in there."

Beth's ears pricked up, she gave the children a problem to solve then joined the maid in the bedroom.

"Let me help," she said. "Why is he so touchy about that?"

"I dunno, he always has been. I never heard them say anyfing strange."

"You heard them talk?" Beth asked, as if they were sharing some great conspiracy.

"Don't tell no one!"

"I won't breathe a word."

"You can 'ear 'em as plain as day in the linen cupboard."

Beth introduced afternoon naps to the children and when one of those coincided with a visit or it happened in the evening she slipped out of her room and into the closet. She listened to half a dozen conversations until…

"We sail on the thirtieth," a gruff voice said.

"That's perfect, I will have the shipping list for the next month by then."

"Good, the lads will be ready. We have four ships now and can take the bigger ones."

"Concentrate on the ones with valuable cargos, we don't need to have to get rid of cheap stuff, there's no profit in it. What about the slaves?"

Beth couldn't believe her luck!

"The Brazilians and Dutch are still buying them and we still have a few customers on the islands."

"What are the prices like?"

"They are getting more expensive, the bloody traders 'ave got greedy now the market is shrinkin'"

"But the owners are willing to pay more?"

"We've started buying to order now. Auctions are done with."

"Good, so we maintain our margin."

"But we have more effort up front, and we have to take into account the death rate."

Beth's hand closed around the butt of the pistol in a holster on her thigh. Like her father she abhorred slavery.

Sunday was her day off and she left the house to walk into town. She met Felix and Hound in a pub well away from both the house and the office.

"It looks like our man is only using the shipping agency as a front. He owns ships used by a team of pirates who are using the South American privateers as cover. Those same men are also actively involved in the slave trade."

"That explains why the same ships turn up at the end of a month every time. They get here in time to collect the next month's shipping list," Felix said.

"Have you searched his study yet?" Hound asked.

"Not yet. I was waiting to talk to you and see if there is anything specific you want me to look for," Beth replied.

"Names and home ports of the ships he owns, names of captains, a ledger with earnings in," Hound said.

"A list of the types of goods they target would be useful too," Felix added.

"Looks like I'm going to have a sleepless night."

Beth chose a night when Jones got home late after a meeting with the guild. He was drunk and his snores resonated. She slipped from her room and, avoiding squeaky floorboards, made her way to the study door. A few seconds of work picked the lock slowed a little by taking care not to scratch the face plate.

Once inside she took off her shawl, used it to block the gap under the door and a lump of wax to block the keyhole. Then she drew the curtains and lit a lamp.

The desk was her first target and she systematically searched it. She found a few interesting papers and noted their contents in a notebook. Then she turned her attention to the cupboards. The first held neatly ordered manifests sorted by ship and date. She noted the ships' names and a sample of the cargos. That took two hours. It was now three in the morning. As the children would wake up at six, she decided that three hours' sleep was better than no sleep. She would come back tomorrow night.

The next night Jones stayed up late doing paperwork. Beth waited until he went to bed and started snoring before she continued the search. She searched the desk again in case he had left anything in it then moved onto the second cabinet. It held absolutely nothing of interest.

Where are you hiding your ledger?

She stood in the middle of the room and looked at the walls, floor, and ceiling. Seeing nothing she moved the lamp to the window and looked again.

Her trained eye scanned the floor.

Nothing.

She knelt and lowered her eyeline as far as she could. The floor was well made and even. Except for one corner that was a fraction of an inch higher.

Aha!

She ran her hands over the section, it was definitely a tenth of an inch higher, but how did it open? She tried digging her fingernails in and lifting. It didn't budge. She knelt on her heels and twiddled a lock of hair thinking of all the ways she would build a secret hideaway. She ran her hands along the skirting board. The builder had come up short in the corner and added a piece to finish the wall.

Or had he?

She gently pressed it.

Didn't move.

She put her fingers on the top edge and pushed down.

Click!

The section of floor rose up.

Clever, spring loaded.

She lifted the section clear and there inside was a ledger with a tied bundle of letters on top. It was the letters that had stopped the top from fitting flush.

She took the ledger and letters to the table and copied the last two pages of the ledger into her notebook. It was a damning account of slave trading and piracy. The letters were also interesting as they were in code. She chose one at random and copied it verbatim. She would decode it later.

Satisfied she had enough for now she put everything back precisely as it had been and replaced the panel which closed with a click. It was 4 am when she fell, exhausted, into her bed.

Hunter and Felix were fascinated by her notes when she handed them over. She had decrypted the letter. It used a substitution cipher based on a keyword, in this case Mulato.

ABC DEFGH I J KLMNOPQR S TUVWXYZAB CD EF

MULATOABCDE FG H I JKLM NOPQ RST UVWXYZ

The key word was the fifth word in the first, unencrypted, sentence.

"He is a busy boy. Regular slave runs with his ships between raids on commerce. Whether he owns the ships or not can be established when we take down his operation," Hunter said.

"Won't that alert the captains?" Beth said.

"No, because by that time we will have substituted the real shipping list for one that leads them into a trap. We will present them with a prize they will not be able to resist taking."

"By we, I suppose you mean me and when do you intend to do it?"

"The end of this month. Why? Are you in a hurry?"

"The coronation is on the 19th July and I have to be there."

Felix looked at her surprised. They didn't know her true identity.

"I suppose you have an invite?" Hunter said sarcastically.

"That is none of your business, but I will have this phase over by then."

"Alright, we will target the end of June list for July. I will coordinate that with T," Hunter said.

"And I will make sure he gets our list, not the real one," Felix added. "You don't need to do anything except verify he has swallowed the bait."

One of his captains arrived on schedule and Beth ensconced herself in the linen cupboard.

After a preamble about trade and what had happened up to then, the captain asked, "You have the list?"

"Yes, and it has a plum in it that you will want to pick."

"Oh yea? What's that?"

"The Venturer leaves Liverpool on the twenty-seventh of July. I've looked into her and she is a converted frigate owned by the Stockley shipping line. She will take a cargo of general goods to Jamaica where she will load coffee."

"Coffee? That's not interesting."

"Ahh but she goes from there to Veracruz where she picks up two tons of prime cochineal and rose wood."

"Two tons! That's worth a fortune!"

"Yes, and the coffee will fetch a good price as well as it's from the Stockley's own Blue Mountain estate.

"You say she's a former frigate. What's her armament?"

"Ten nine-pounders to a side."

"And crew?"

"One hundred men."

"That's a lot."

"Not enough to fight both sides and sail her."

"To be sure of taking her we would need all four schooners."

"She will be worth the effort. I bet she will be carrying bullion too."

Three days later Beth left the Jones's employment stating that there had been a family bereavement and that she had to go back to Sheffield. The children cried as they had grown to like her. It tugged at her heartstrings as well as she knew that the future was not rosy for the family and she was fond of them too.

Pomp and Ceremony

Beth arrived at the family house on the twelfth of July to find her family at home. Her father, tanned and as handsome as ever. Her mother had a delicate shading to her skin that told of her care in protecting it from the sun. James was as brown as Father.

She and James would attend the coronation along with the twins who would arrive soon. Unlike her parents who would have formal robes to wear they would dress in normal evening dress. That is the girls in ball gowns and the boys in top hats and tails or dress uniform.

Beth was more interested in meeting with Admiral Turner. 'T', had sent her a message to report to his office and when she arrived, she was surprised to see Captain Ackermann there as well.

"I thought you were in Greece?"

"The recall message arrived a week after your father and mother left for home. I got here yesterday."

"Just in time," Turner said. "Chaton, please brief the good captain on your mission."

Beth gave Wolfgang a succinct account of the mission and the results so far.

"Aah, you want to use the Unicorn as the trap," Wolfgang said.

"Exactly," Turner said. "Now this is how it is going to work. You will rename as the Venturer and offload all but one hundred of your men at Chatham who will board the Queen Charlotte. You will then sail to Liverpool and take on a cargo of commercial goods. Chaton will join the ship there. She will be leaving as herself ostensibly to visit their plantation."

Oh, goodie a Caribbean cruise!

"You will sail on the twenty-seventh for Jamaica and will rendezvous with the Queen Charlotte twenty miles off Cork to re-embark your men. In Jamaica you will behave as a merchantman and offload your cargo at Kingston. You will take on a load of coffee and what will appear to be bullion, then leave for Veracruz. There you will pick up more cargo for the return trip to England. Cochineal and Rosewood."

"They will probably watch you leave port and set an ambush between Cuba and Florida," Beth said.

"Then we will give them a warm welcome," Wolfgang grinned.

"Chaton, you are to stay in Veracruz. You will need to speak Spanish. I believe you started learning in the academy?"

"Yes. What am I to do there?"

"We have an agent, codename Troupial, who I want you to work with to establish if there are any other British- American- or European-owned ships involved in piracy." He passed her a packet. "Here are your briefing notes." He passed Wolfgang another, "And here are your orders."

"Captain, do you have any Spanish speaking sailors aboard?"

"Not that I know of, but your father has the Basques. Maybe he can spare one for this mission?"

"That is a good idea," Turner said. "Let him know that I have approved the assignment of one of them to this mission. I am sure he will be happy."

Beth met her parents at the family home in Grosvenor Square.

"You have another mission already?" her mother said, disappointed that her little girl was leaving again so soon.

"It's part of the same one, just following through at the other end."

"You need to perfect your Spanish," her father said. He was very aware of her capabilities and skills.

"Wolfgang suggested one of the Shadows accompany me to help with that, and T has approved the assignment of one to this mission."

Her father tried not to look too pleased at that. She was his little girl after all and one of his crack team of men would help keep his and her mother's minds at rest.

"Any preference?" he asked casually.

Beth wasn't fooled.

"Not Matai, he is your team's medical man. It's between Antton and Garai."

"They both speak Spanish, French and Basque. Garai is the better investigator, Antton is a good leader and the best climber."

"That's because he comes from the mountains outside Bilbao. I will take Garai if that is alright with you."

Her mother looked happier now that she had someone she trusted with her own life alongside Beth on the mission.

King George IV's coronation at Westminster Abbey was a lavish affair in keeping with his character and history. He had borrowed widely to pay for it. Beth's father had put up fifty thousand pounds against the king's personal note. Beth considered the chances of him getting it back at little to none. What she didn't know but Marty did, was that the king had access to the war reparations paid by the French. He would be paid back from those.

Her parents were dressed in robes of state befitting their rank and would be part of the procession to the abbey. Beth was escorted by her brother James who was now a lieutenant in the Royal Navy. He was dressed in full uniform with a fore and aft bicorn hat with ostrich plume. She was stunning in a ball gown of iridescent green. The twins were, for once, well behaved and hid any signs of boredom with the whole affair. The fact was that as King George was godfather to all of them, their presence was required, and any misbehaviour would not only reflect on them and their parents but on him as well. They were seated in the newly erected tiered seats that lined the abbey that would hold the majority of the four thousand guests.

Beth would have preferred to have been escorted by her beau, Sebastian, but he was on duty as part of the honour guard. She saw him and was sure he saw her, but he was too professional to give any indication. The professional in her noted that the Rifles were the only soldiers carrying guns and were in their green uniforms. The rest carried pikes and were in traditional uniforms that dated back to the 16th century.

The king arrived and Beth held in a gasp, he was huge! They had tried to tame his fat belly with a corset but that had just pushed the fat down and he looked strange and misshapen.

All of the official paintings would show a svelte king in good shape posing coolly for the artist. He was in fact sweating heavily.

The coronation plodded through to the end of the ceremony at around half past three and the worthies filed out to proceed back to Westminster Hall for the banquet. Beth and James were invited but the twins not as they were deemed too young.

Beth endured the heat generated by two thousand candles and twenty-six vast chandeliers, but she drew the line at having hot wax drip on her and pulled a shawl over her head to protect herself. At last it was over and she could leave along with James. Her parents were to accompany the king to Charlton House and waved to her as they followed the king out.

The siblings made their way from the hall to where their carriage was waiting. It was stuck in a jam of carriages and onlookers who had swarmed the road. Beth blew out her cheeks.

"Can I help?" a familiar voice said from behind them.

Beth turned and fell into the arms of Sebastian. James waited patiently for them to come up for air.

"How did you find us?" Beth breathed. She was somewhat breathless.

"I found your carriage when I came off duty and just waited. I don't think it's going anywhere."

"It's only a mile to the house, why don't we walk?" James said.

Beth agreed "That's a good idea. We will be home well before this mess sorts itself out."

They gave instructions for the driver to return home when he could and started out. They stayed to the main roads and strolled rather than walked fast as the streets were full of celebrating people. They walked along Whitehall to Pall Mall and then up St James Street to Park Lane. Two obviously military men armed with swords was enough to keep the footpads at bay.

They arrived at the house thirty minutes after they left. The windows were bright with light and a party was in full swing. The servants and their families had been given permission by Lord Martin to celebrate the coronation in their own way. Music was being provided by Melissa, who played piano, and Matai who played a pipe and tambor. James went straight to Melissa and sat beside her at the piano. Sebastian grabbed Beth and launched into a spirited fandango when Matai started a tune from his homeland. They had plenty of room as the drawing room had been largely cleared of furniture. Antton grabbed Tabetha and joined in. Soon the whole room was laughing and dancing or clapping along.

Beth's parents, Marty and Caroline, got home to find the party still in full flow at midnight. Servants from adjoining houses had joined and stopped and gawped at the seriously overdressed peers. Marty grinned, waved then ran upstairs to get changed. He had had enough pomp and ceremony.

The Stockley household was very quiet the next morning. Sebastian and Beth had shared a bed as did James and Melissa. Marty and Caroline crept downstairs to avoid waking anyone else and were surprised when they entered the dining room to find both couples already there.

"Morning Daddy, Mama. Did you sleep well?" Beth said.

"Yes, thank you," Caroline said, kicking Marty who was about to make a facetious comment.

"My lord, may I have a moment of your time after breakfast?" Sebastian said. The twins giggled as they came in and heard.

Marty went to the sideboard and helped himself to a large cup of coffee and a plate of bacon, poached eggs, kidneys, black pudding, and potatoes fried in the bacon fat. Topping it off with three slices of thick toast and a slab of butter he returned to the table.

"After I've eaten this."

Caroline rolled her eyes.

"My lord." Sebastian shuffled his feet awkwardly.

"You have been calling me Martin since Waterloo, spit it out, man."

"Martin," Sebastian said with a shy smile, "I have come to ask for Beth's hand in marriage."

"Thought as much. As you have been defiling my daughter for the last month or so you can do no less than make an honest woman of her." Martin glared at him.

Sebastian was aghast and it showed on his face. Marty burst out laughing.

"Serves you right, you should have asked earlier. Of course, you can."

Sebastian almost fell over in relief. Then found his hand being pumped as Martin shook it.

The door burst open, and an outraged Beth charged in and was swept up in Marty's arms before she could get more than "Daddy how—" She had been listening at the door.

He put her down and held her at arm's length.

"You finally caught him. Took you long enough. Congratulations!"

Caroline came in and hugged them both.

"When Beth is twenty-one, we can have the ceremony in Saint Georges."

Beth turned to her father, "Daddy but—"

"No buts. Your mother needs time to organise everything."

"A year and a half?"

"Who knows you may not get back from this mission until then."

Sebastian looked at her questioningly.

"I was going to tell you this evening. They are sending me to South America."

"Damn, so soon. Is anyone going with you?"

"We are sending Garai with her," Marty said.

"One of the Shadows? Then she will be in good hands."

Sebastian had leave for three days. One of the things he wanted to do was introduce Beth to his parents. Cropley Ashley-Cooper was the 6th Earl of Shaftesbury and a member of the House of Lords where he was Chairman of Committees.

His wife, Lady Anne, was a Spencer. Beth was very nervous when they pulled up at their London house.

Sebastian was dressed, for once, in civilian clothes and when the door opened the footman did a double take before he recognised him.

"My Lord, welcome home," he said.

"Hello, Thackery, are my parents at home?"

"They are in the drawing room."

He took Beth, who was dressed in her best, and led her through the door into the elegant hallway. Large double doors that must have been contemporary with the rest of the 17th century building led them into the drawing room. The earl and countess were sat in comfortable chairs, him reading the paper and her doing needlepoint.

The earl looked up as they entered.

"Sebastian, good morning. You are out of uniform. On leave?" Then he saw Beth and his eyebrows rose. "And who is this?"

The countess, who was a little hard of hearing, turned to see who her husband was talking to. Her face lit up and stood, her arms out. Sebastian embraced her then moved to his father who shook his hand.

"Who is this?" the countess asked.

"Mother, Father, may I present the Right Honourable Bethany Stockley, my fiancée."

"Well, you were worth waiting for," the earl said out loud.

Sebastian rolled his eyes and Beth had to suppress a giggle.

"Father has a habit of thinking out loud," Sebastian said.

The countess came to her and took both her hands,

"I knew he was waiting for someone since he came back from France. You will make a wonderful couple."

"I am so pleased to meet you," Beth said.

"Stockley? Your father is Viscount Stockley?" the Earl said.

"Yes, my lord."

"He's been busy in Greece I hear."

"He was. He came home for the coronation."

"I saw him there."

"We will shop for rings this afternoon," Sebastian said heading off further comment.

"And lockets," Beth added.

"What about the dowry?" the earl said.

"Lord Martin is not insisting on one," Sebastian said.

"Don't need one?" the earl spluttered.

"Dear, I am sure Bethany is quite well provided for," the countess interjected.

Beth couldn't tell them she was a salaried member of the secret service, as even one as high ranked in government as the   earl, weren't told who the agents were.

"I am, my lady, my father has created trusts for all his children so the property can remain intact after his passing."

"Call me Anne, dear."

The ladies went off to chat leaving the men alone.

"Her father is in the Intelligence Service you know."

"I do, I have fought with him when he was Wellington's chief of intelligence. He is a formidable warrior."

"Made his fortune before he met Lady Caroline an' all."

"Indeed."

"She's a good catch."

"I have loved her since the first time I met her in France."

The earl was not interested in that.

"How old is she?"

"Nineteen, she will be twenty in October."

The earl frowned. "She was fifteen when you met?"

"Thereabouts. Actually, fifteen going on twenty."

"Girls mature faster than boys."

"They certainly do."

"I spoke to Wellington yesterday."

"Oh? What did he have to say?"

"That he was very pleased with you." The earl looked slightly shy saying that as he wasn't one to give easy praise. "When will the blessing of the engagement be?"

"Sunday week. Beth is leaving for the Caribbean on the twenty-seventh."

"What? Why is she going to that God-forsaken place?"

"Her family have plantations; she is going to inspect them."

"Women, messing around in commerce. It's not natural."

Sebastian had heard that before.

"We will marry in November next year. Lady Caroline will organise everything while Beth is away."

His father looked at him suspiciously.

"You seem damn casual about your betrothed swanning off for months."

"She has her duty as I have mine," he said, in a tone that closed that particular thread of conversation.

They went to Garrard's in Bond Street to purchase their rings and pendants. As was the style of the time the rings were actually two halves of what would be Beth's wedding ring. Cunningly designed and engraved with symbols and words of love they would wear half each until their wedding day when the two halves would be reunited into one ring. They chose the words carefully and the master jeweller took the rings to his workshop to engrave. In the meantime, they looked at pendants.

"We want matching gold pendants. One with a neck chain, the other to be clipped to a watch chain," Beth told the salesperson.

The young man pulled out a tray from behind the counter and laid it on the top.

"These are paired for the newly betrothed. You can put a portrait on one side and a lock of hair behind glass on the other."

"Do you have an artist who can do the portraits?" Sebastian asked.

"Certainly, my lord. You can choose from George Engleheart and John Smart."

"Engleheart is very good," Beth said "Mother has a portrait of Father by him."

"When can we sit for him?" Sebastian asked.

"I will enquire and let you know. He is very busy, but I am sure he will fit you in as soon as possible."

"We need him to start them before the twenty-fifth as we will be separated for some time after that."

"I am sure that will be possible."

Beth had been studying the lockets.

"I like these," she said and held up a pair that were oval, about an inch long by three quarters wide, with a cartouche where a name could be engraved.

"They are very nice. I'll buy you one if you buy me one," Sebastian smiled.

They sat for their portraits two days later. The chance to immortalise two people from such high-ranked families was enough of an incentive for Engleheart. Even then the process would take six months. Beth would sit again before she left but after that the artist would have to work from a portrait that had been done a year earlier.

The twenty-fifth came around and she was packed and ready to leave. Sebastian said his goodbyes the night before and she was a little bleary eyed when she, her lady's maid, Sandra, and Garai got in the coach. Her mother had not made a fuss and her father had hugged her and told her to be careful. Once they were on the road, she put her professional head on.

"You must call me Beth," she told Garai and Carole. "No miladys or ma'ams when we are in Mexico."

"Of course," Garai answered with a completely straight face.

"I'm teaching you how to suck eggs, aren't I?"

"Not at all, it's better to be clear, but I am supposed to be your servant so Miss Beth may be better in public." Carole just nodded. She knew what Beth was as she had been selected and vetted by the Intelligence Service.

"Yes of course," Beth said, a little chagrined.

He took out an apple and a curved knife, carved a chunk off and popped it in his mouth. "What is this?" he said in Spanish.

"A knife but I am not familiar with it," she replied in kind.

"It is an Indonesian Karambit. It can be used as a general tool or for fighting." He flipped it around, so he gripped it in his fist the curved blade facing forward and pointing down. "You hold it like this."

"It would be very good for slashing."

"It is and the chances are your opponent will never have seen one before. Which will give you an advantage."

He flipped it around and sliced off another chunk of apple which he offered to Beth. She took it and munched on it.

"You look like you could do with some sleep."

"I could if you don't mind."

"Please, go ahead. I will keep watch."

The Venturer

Wolfgang, with one hundred men aboard, navigated his disguised frigate out of the Medway into the English Channel. She was not officially a navy ship, being part of the Intelligence Service's mobile unit otherwise known as the Special Operations Flotilla. The Queen Charlotte had left two days before to sail around the south coasts of England and Ireland to the rendezvous. Her decks full of the Unicorn's one hundred and fifty sailors and thirty marines. She was infamous for having had a black woman serving onboard disguised as a man. William Brown was 'discovered' in 1815 and discharged from the service. The Unicorns made a point of jokingly checking each man they met.

Once out in open water the Unicorn changed into the Venturer and flew the red ensign. Her eighteen-pound guns were covered, and the huge carronades mounted on the foredeck centreline were hidden by a shed-like structure that could be collapsed in a few seconds. The officers and crew wore civilian clothes just like any other merchant crew. Shanties were sung as they hauled on the lines accompanied by a fiddler who sat on the top of the capstan. It was all very un-navy like.

The Ventura took a deep sweep around the south coast to stay out of sight of land and up the west coast of Ireland to enter the Irish Sea from the north. They spotted the Queen Charlotte on her station, ostensibly patrolling the Atlantic approaches, and entered Liverpool roughly on time. They moored up at Nelson Dock where her cargo and Bethany should be waiting for them.

Wolfgang handled the ship like a merchantman, professionally but not to the precise standards of the navy. The story was they had come from a refit, which is why they were empty. The Stockley fleet was notorious amongst the merchant community for being well maintained and only carrying high-value cargo back from the Caribbean and elsewhere.

They didn't have to wait long for the cargo to arrive and then a carriage pulled up with the Stockley arms on its doors. Garai stepped out and helped Bethany down. A maid followed. Porters ran to offload her luggage and were generously tipped by Garai on her behalf. She looked every bit the lady and behaved as one would expect the daughter of Lady Caroline. Friendly but cool, polite while maintaining her distance. It brought back memories of the past when Martin and Caroline fought side by side on his quarterdeck. But that was another time and another ship.

He greeted her at the top of the gangplank.

"Permission to come aboard, Captain?" she said with a dazzling smile.

"Permission granted," he said, playing along.

She stepped onto the deck and curtsied, he bent over her hand with a bow.

"It's good to see you, Wolfgang," Garai said from behind her.

"You too, my friend."

They shook hands after Beth stepped aside.

"I have had the men construct cabins on the gun deck. It is where the extra marines would normally bunk but we are only carrying thirty for this trip."

The porters were waiting at the bottom of the gangplank to bring the baggage aboard, but Wolfgang didn't want them on his ship, so a net was lowered and it was loaded with that. Sailors took it below.

Beth found a nicely appointed cabin with the usual amenities including a commode, washstand, and a place to hang her dresses. The cot was big enough for one and had fresh linen and blankets on a comfortable mattress. She went up on deck in time to see the last of the cargo loaded.

As she scanned the dock, she saw a face she recognised standing by a warehouse. It was Jones. She wore a broad, floppy-brimmed hat that put her face in shadow, so he wouldn't recognise her. He was intent on watching the ship and didn't see Felix watching him from where he sat on a stack of crates some thirty yards away. They would leave him alone for now but when the Venturer returned to Liverpool he would be taken and charged.

A water hoy came alongside, and they topped off the water tanks. The fore deck manger was fully occupied with quail, rabbits, chickens (for eggs), a pair of pigs, six piglets, and a pair of goats. The ship's surgeon, Mr Shelby, was onboard and met her on the deck.

"Miss Bethany, you are looking radiant as ever."

"Hello, Shelby, how is Annabelle?"

"Glowing with health, she has passed her second trimester. She has decided she wants to give birth on shore, so stayed in London."

"You didn't want to deliver it yourself?"

"If we are back in time I will, but the midwife we have chosen is modern and competent, so I am content."

Orders were shouted, the watering was finished and the watermen had pulled their boats up to haul the Venturer out into the stream. Beth and Shelby watched as the top men ran up to remove the harbour gaskets in preparation for setting sail. She noticed Garai amongst them. At almost fifty years old he was still as fit and agile as the best of them.

That made her pause for thought as the idea that the Shadows were all getting on a bit and must be getting close to retiring or at least taking positions at the academy. She started thinking that having her own team wouldn't be such a bad idea.

The watermen did their job and Wolfgang tossed a small purse down to tip them. They would divide it up amongst themselves. It wasn't much but it kept the Stockley brand in good stead. The jibs, staysails and spanker were set as the wind was from the southwest and too fine for the square sails.

They were going with the current, so the land slid by at around six knots or seven miles an hour. They were soon out of the city and farmland dominated the riverbanks. Beth stood at the rail and watched it pass; she knew it was the last she would see of England for a while.

Garai appeared, "All's well?" he said in Spanish. He had told her that they would only converse in Spanish for the entire crossing as she needed to be fluent with a natural accent by the time they got to Mexico.

The topsails boomed as they dropped, followed by the mains as they turned north to sail up the Irish Sea past the Isle of Man. Their speed increased and a fine bow wave adorned the prow. One of the crew came to her, "Milady, there are dolphins at the bow if you care to come see."

Beth was delighted to 'come see' and marvelled at the sleek grey mammals she had seen only in the Mediterranean before. They rode the bow wave with no apparent effort. One leapt into the air, turning its body and looked right at her. She was convinced it had just said hello.

"Marvellous animals, are they not?" Shelby said.

"They are so agile and seem to be quite intelligent."

"I read in the journal of the Royal Academy, that they have bigger brains than ours, but it seems to be more divided."

"Really? So, they could be intelligent?"

"We would have to capture some and study them in captivity to assess that."

The thought of these magnificent animals being held in a zoo was repugnant.

"They need their freedom. Look at them."

"They do enjoy playing, that is for sure."

They watched the dolphins until the animals left them by which time they were passing the Isle of Man on their port side.

Beth was enjoying the summer sunshine and stayed on deck until they entered the Atlantic where it got a lot rougher. It was time to change for dinner anyway, so she went to her cabin. She was a good sailor, which couldn't be said for Sandra.

"I feel awful, Milady. This bobbin' up and down is making me feel all queasy."

Beth took pity on her and put her to bed with a bowl. The sea wasn't that big and the motion was just up and down. She could imagine that if they hit a storm coming in across the Atlantic, Sandra would be disabled.

Dinner was in the captain's cabin and was a simple three-course meal. Shelby and McGivern, the first lieutenant, attended. Wolfgang had his own cook, a newly-recruited Italian he had found in Malta. The man had a shady past and had begged to be signed on as he was being hunted by both the police and the criminal fraternity. He was, however, an excellent chef.

The soup was a rich chicken broth thickened with bread, Tuscan style, with delicious pieces of spicy sausage in it. The main dish was veal, fried in butter and herbs served with a cream sauce, rosemary baked potatoes and greens. The pudding, a marvellous mixture of sponge soaked in coffee, covered in thick whipped cream and sprinkled with chocolate.

Afterwards, they sat and drank coffee.

"How is Sandra?" Shelby asked.

"I had some chicken soup sent down. Garai is looking after her."

"He's still single, isn't he?"

"Yes, but you need not fear for her virtue, Garai is a gentleman."

"I know and he isn't interested in women," Wolfgang said. "He has hidden it well over the years, but your father and the rest of the Shadows have known for a long time."

"He is a homosexual?" Beth said, astonished.

"He would prefer to be referred to as celibate," Shelby said.

"I had no idea."

"Is it a problem?" Wolfgang said.

"No, I have no prejudice one way or the other, but I am sad he has never found love."

"He may one day. My gunner has and look at him."

Wolverton, the ship's master gunner, was a misshapen dwarf of a man with short legs, a barrel chest and long, extremely strong, arms. Everyone knew he had a boyfriend but the two were circumspect, didn't bother anyone else and the crew treated them with respect. *Mind, Father's ships are probably the only ones in the navy they could get away with that on,* Beth thought.

They rendezvoused with the Queen Charlotte that evening at dusk and their men reboarded. Both the crew of the Charlotte and their men were relieved to be back to normal and a party atmosphere grew as the men were reunited with their mates. Wolfgang spliced the mainbrace, and the ship soon rang with the sound of pipes, a drum, and the fiddler playing a raunchy shanty. The men sang and danced. The sound of their feet stamping on the deck could be heard below. Beth smiled until it was replaced with the sound of Sandra retching.

Sandra finally got her sea legs a week into the voyage and that created another problem. She was a flirt. She enjoyed talking to the men and flirted outrageously and a couple of them thought she was serious. A fight broke out and the two men had to be disciplined.

"Sandra, you caused this so you will have to face up to the consequences," Beth told her. "They fought over you and will face punishment because of you."

The men were brought before Captain Ackermann the next morning. Beth dragged Sandra on to the quarterdeck to witness what happened next.

"You are charged with fighting. Looking at your faces I can see that it was quite a serious one. Do you have anything to say for yourselves?"

Both men shook their heads.

"Divisional commanders, do you have anything to say in their defence?"

Midshipman Stirling stepped forward. "Benjamin Grimes is rated able and a topman on the foremast. He has been on the ship for four years and to now has had a clean record. He is industrious and an excellent sailor in all respects."

Midshipman Hepworth stepped forward, "Archibald Greeves is rated able and a member of the afterguard. He has been punished once for being drunk on duty but since then has conducted himself in an exemplary fashion. He is a willing and hard worker."

Wolfgang deliberated. "Given your previous conduct I am disappointed that you decided to resolve your differences with your fists. I am aware of the cause but that is even less an excuse than any other I can think of. You will both be served twelve strokes of the cat to be served immediately. Rig a grating."

Beth stood behind Sandra, a hand in her hair to stop her looking away. She was angry enough to beat some sense into the silly minx. She could feel her shake as she watched the crew prepare the men for punishment. Their shirts were removed, and Shelby tied leather aprons around their waists to protect their kidneys. He checked both men and declared them fit to receive punishment. Ben Grimes was first and was brought forward to have his wrists and ankles tied to the grating. A pair of bosun's mates took up position and removed the cats from their red velvet bags. One right-handed the other left, they would deliver half the strokes each.

The cats were made by the mates. Punishment was so rare on the Unicorn that they made some to keep their hands in so had a few on hand. Neither Commodore Stockley or Wolfgang approved of knotting the tails as they considered that the tails did enough damage on their own.

The mates ran their fingers through the tails to make sure they were not tangled. "Lay on," Wolfgang commanded.

The first stroke was delivered. Sandra cried out. Beth was relentless and forced her to watch. After six, blood was flowing, and the mates changed. The first strike was delivered creating a chequered pattern. Ben groaned once, then stiffened up and made no further sound.

Sandra was crying and Beth said in her ear, "Do you understand now?"

Sandra sobbed, "Yes."

Archi was brought forward. He was twenty-five years old and had never faced punishment before. It didn't help that he had seen Ben being punished. He was no coward, he had faced the French towards the end of the war and the Ottomans more recently, but the prospect of the cat almost unmanned him.

The marines who brought him forward, held him up by his elbows. He managed to stand for his wrists to be lashed. Shelby, a good judge of a man's qualities, placed a leather strip between his teeth. The punishment commenced but even having witnessed Ben's didn't prepare him for the utter agony that built up stroke by stroke. By the end he had to be almost carried below for Shelby to treat.

Beth made Sandra watch to the bitter end. Then marched her down to her cabin.

"You are extremely privileged to be on this ship. Learn from this and treat the men with respect. If I catch you flirting again, I will personally take a cat to you. Do you understand?"

"Yes, Ma'am."

Beth left her in her cabin and returned to her own.

"That was a hard lesson," Garai said from where he had been waiting for her.

"She had to see what the consequences of her actions were, she is thoughtless, not callous."

There was a knock on the door. It was Sandra.

"Miss Beth, can I ask if it's possible for me to see those boys and apologise?"

"If Garai goes with you. What will you tell them?"

"That I am a silly ninny, that I was playing a stupid game and I am sorry they got into trouble for it."

"They have to take some of the blame as well. They both knew better than to fight aboard ship," Garai said.

Beth gave him a look out the side of her eye. He ignored it and led the girl down to the Orlop deck. When they returned, she had been crying again, and went to her room.

Princess Beth

Six and a half weeks after leaving Liverpool they anchored in Kingston. The Stockley's long-term agent Malakai Norwood III came aboard not long after they got there.

"An unusual ship for the Stockley Company," he observed as he looked around.

"It's chartered," Beth replied.

"All the same, an unusual ship indeed, and a lot of crew."

"Mr Norwood, you know my mother and father," Beth said, as if lecturing a child.

"Of course."

"Then you know better than to ask questions."

"Aah, I see," he said, nodding sagely.

"While the cargo is being unloaded, I would like to visit our plantations and have a look at the one you are recommending we buy. Mother said something about historical connections."

"Quite so, Miss Bethany. The property was once owned by the notorious privateer, The Scarlett Fox. Her real name was Scarlett Browning."

"Good Lord! I have read her journal. She was my great, times six, grandmother. Didn't she also own the estate in the mountains?"

"She did indeed. This one is further towards the coast and is a cocoa plantation. I believe in her day it was called The Den."

"There was a plantation called that. It's not far from Annotto Bay isn't it?"

"It is indeed. There is a good road these days down the coast. We can be there by carriage in a few hours."

They went ashore where Malakai had a landau waiting. He had packed a picnic hamper, so they set off straight away. Beth anointed herself with citronella oil to fend off the worst of the mosquitoes and had a parasol to protect her from the harsh sun.

That day there was a good breeze blowing from the northeast off the sea which both cooled and blew the mosquitoes away, making the trip quite pleasant. The horses were well cared for and fit and happily trotted at a fair pace. They reached the gates of the plantation. The current ones were showing signs of age and the name board above them was unreadable. The carriage slid under it and as they entered Beth shuddered as goosebumps came up on her skin.

"Are you alright?" Malakai asked.

Beth closed her eyes and felt a presence. The feeling wore off as soon as it came. She opened her eyes, "Yes. I just felt like someone was watching me."

She frowned, it was different from when she was being physically watched. The feeling had been gentler almost like a recognition. The drive passed between ancient fruit-tree orchards with bushes growing beneath them.

"The cocoa beans originate from the rain forests. They do much better when shaded under trees," Malakai said.

"What fruits are growing here?"

"Mango, ackee and breadfruit. There are also moringa trees."

"So, they get more than one crop?"

"The fruit is sold locally; they are all popular."

The house came into view. A single-story colonial style mansion with a porch that ran around three sides. On the porch were wicker or rattan chairs, some of them rockers. She remembered an entry in the journal that described the day Scarlett fell in love with Stephen. He drew a picture of her on this very porch. The picture came from his heart as well as his eye and was so full of feeling that Scarlett fell in love with him there and then.

A man and woman came out of the house to meet them as they disembarked from the landau. Malakai greeted them.

"Mr and Mrs Flanigan, so nice to see you. May I introduce the Right Honourable Bethany Stockley. Her father Viscount Stockley and mother are interested in acquiring the plantation."

"Why are you selling?" Beth asked. After polite greetings had been made.

"We have had this plantation in our family for three generations but now our daughter is not interested in continuing with it after us," Mr Flanigan said.

"May I see inside the house?"

"Of course, Martha will show you around."

Beth got the impression that Martha didn't see many people aside from Mr Flannigan. She chatted nineteen to the dozen and bounced from subject to subject randomly. Beth let it wash over her and concentrated on the house and what she could feel. It felt welcoming. Her instincts were all crying out to her that this was – home?

She took a deep breath when she entered the master bedroom. It was just as Scarlett had described in her journal, she walked to the window and looked out into the yard. That was where she had rescued Gavin from being whipped. She wasn't sure whether she was reflecting the journal, or the feelings came from somewhere else.

"Can I see the cellar?"

"What a strange one you are," Martha said. She had stopped talking a while ago, without Beth noticing.

The steps down to the basement stopped at a thick door made of oak with iron bands. It was heavy and the lock was large and strong. She pushed it open.

"Do you have a candle?" she asked.

Light was provided and she went further in. She went to the far wall. It had been plastered.

There should be another door here.

She said nothing and went back up to the ground floor.

She went through the estate accounts and satisfied herself that it was profitable. Then they left the house and walked out through the grounds. There was an overgrown area that drew her to it.

"Why is this area so overgrown?"

"Oh, the workers won't go in there," Martha said, "they say it's got bad juju. Ghosts or spirits are said to haunt it."

"It was a graveyard," Beth said quietly.

"What? How could you ever know that?"

Beth didn't answer but walked forward and tried to push the undergrowth aside. It was too thick, and she resolved she would do something about that.

"How much do they want for it?" she asked Malakai.

"They are asking for six hundred pounds."

"And the workers?"

"That's the catch. None are under contract. This plantation had slaves in name only and was the first to officially free all of them before it was sold off and the Flannigan's bought it. The unusual thing is that most chose to stay."

Beth took off her hat as her head was too hot and her auburn hair shone in the sun. When they visited the area where the workers lived a crowd gathered.

A very old woman came forward and looked at her. She looked at her hair then stepped up and looked at her eyes. Then she walked around her.

"You are related to Miss Scarlett? The stories tell of her and you is the image of her."

"She was my great, great, great, great, great, great grandmother."

"The Lord be praised!" the old woman said and shouted something in Patois. A great excitement took hold of the workers, and they crowded around. "Will you take back what is yours?"

"My mother and father will own the plantation. They own the Stockley plantation in the blue mountains already."

"Your mother looks like you?"

"They say we look like sisters."

Beth wrote a letter to her parents saying she was instructing Malakai to buy the plantation on their behalf. There were sufficient funds in Jamaica to cover it. She told them of the encounter with the old woman and that she had learnt that there was a legend amongst the former slaves that Miss Scarlett would someday return. She was the queen of their tribe and they had been lost since she had left them.

One thing Beth noticed is that they all had the tattoo of an iguana on their hands. She looked at hers and wondered if at some time she would get one as well. She had seen a portrait of Scarlett and knew she looked a bit like her. Same hair and face shape. She imagined herself sailing the Spanish Main capturing ships and raiding cities for loot. She couldn't, however, imagine burning Jesuit priests. Scarlett had never forgiven the inquisition for the death of her first love and had been forever vengeful. Beth wished she could have met the

Indians she wrote about as well but as far as she knew they all died out years ago.

The visit to the Blue Mountain estate was much more normal. Her mother had visited and even lived there at times. The estate manager was Phineas Calthorpe and was extremely competent.

"Welcome, Lady Bethany," he said, smiling broadly.

"Mr Calthorpe, please call me Beth."

"Then you must call me Fin. Welcome to Blue Mountain. It's been a while since we saw a member of the family here."

"We have been remiss. But the war and other business has been keeping us busy. I hope we can be here at least once a year from now on," Beth said, hoping it was her that was sent.

The plantation house here was a more traditional two-story affair. Painted white with a columned porch on the south side. It had an extensive garden planted with exotic flowers and a walled vegetable garden. The estate grew coffee of a very high quality and had a loyal workforce, most of whom had been born on the estate. Like cocoa, coffee plants liked shade, and this plantation was adapted from a pre-existing forest with a scattering of fruit trees introduced to provide for the estate.

The Stockleys and, before them, the Brownings had never approved of slavery and had freed the slaves on their plantations as soon as they could. Before that they had treated the slaves as people, not draft animals or objects. Their slavery was maintained only because they could not legally be freed without running the risk of being taken and forced back into slavery by some other plantation owner.

She was given a tour of the processing sheds. She learnt that the coffee cherries were harvested and hulled to produce the beans. Normally two to a cherry. Every now and then a single bean would be produced called a peaberry. These were separated and processed as they produced a sweeter, more flavoursome coffee which sold for a premium. All the beans were dried after hulling and, when they were ready, graded and packed for shipping. Some were roasted on the estate to monitor the flavour and for the use of the workers. Beth was served a cup of the last crop.

"That is delicious," she sighed as she took a sip of the dark, flavoursome brew. It was not bitter but pleasantly mild.

They brewed it using a pharmacist's pressure vessel like her father did. The girl who operated this beast was Carmen. She was from Columbia and had come to Jamaica as a child with her parents. She had discovered a talent for making coffee and worked at the estate and in a local coffee shop. No wedding, funeral or baptism could be held in the local area without her behind the bar serving coffee and alcohol.

Beth met and interacted with the estate workers and again, there was that tattoo. This time she asked about it. An old man who must have been at least eighty years old was brought forward.

"Miss Beth, your ancestor introduced the mark instead of branding her slaves. It became the symbol of our tribe not a mark of shame. Everyone who can trace their ancestors back to that first group of slaves carries the mark." A little boy came forward and proudly showed her his. "When your mother bought this plantation we found our way back here. She is our queen and you are our princess."

"Do you know of the people at the estate near Annotto Bay?"

"We know that there was a second plantation. We didn't know where it was."

"They also carry the mark."

"Then they are our people."

"I am buying that estate for my mother. We will reunite you."

The party lasted until well into the wee small hours and Beth discovered rum. In the morning she discovered what a real hangover felt like.

"Oh, my god. Why do people do this to themselves? Why did I do this to myself?" she asked the bottom of her third cup of coffee.

"Have you never had a hangover before?" Malakai asked. He was suffering as well.

"No, and I do not want another. Rum is lovely but this…" she left the rest hanging.

They left after lunch. She was feeling better, and her head only hurt if she moved suddenly. The trip back to Kingston was relatively peaceful until they got to Golden Spring. A pair of men were blocking the road with a hand cart.

Malakai shouted at them to clear the road. Beth felt something was wrong and reached into her purse. A third man stepped out of the bushes at the side of the road. Scruffy, five feet four, receding hairline, broken nose, and a squint, all registered immediately with Beth along with the ancient pistol he was holding.

"Is that the best you have?" she said and pulled her double-barrelled Lill pistol, cocking it with her thumb. The man raised his pistol and looked quite surprised as her first shot hit him precisely between the eyes. She didn't wait to see him fall but turned the second barrel into line, automatically checking the percussion cap with her thumb. She pointed it at the other two men.

"It's good you brought the cart, you can take his body away in it. Now if you don't want to join him, get the hell out of our way. I have a ship to catch."

The men were in shock and numbly moved the cart to the side. Malakai flicked the reins and the horses moved forward, anxious to get away from the smell of death. Beth watched the men approach the corpse where one fell to his knees and howled a cry of loss.

"I think I killed his brother."

The Fox

The Venturer glided into the harbour at Veracruz. A pilot came aboard, and they were guided past the fort of Sant Juan de Ulúa towards a dock. Beth looked at the ancient structure.

"Those cannons look to be as old as the fort," she said to Wolfgang, who was scanning them with a telescope as a matter of routine.

"Brass twenty-four-pounders. They may be old but they can still throw a ball."

He lowered the telescope and scanned the harbour. In the background the pilot gave the helm an order.

"Those two schooners over there look out of place," he said and examined them with the telescope. "Badly concealed guns on their main decks."

"Can you see the names?" Beth said.

"One is," he paused as he adjusted the focus, "the Genevieve. I cannot see the name of the other."

"That's one of James' ships. Odds are the other is his as well."

"We will get you ashore and load the cargo, then we can spring the trap."

Beth looked up at him and smiled. "Didn't I tell you?"

Wolfgang knew what was coming, she was her mother and father's daughter through and through.

"You are staying aboard."

"You spoiled the surprise," she pouted.

"Young lady, the day you surprise me I shall run naked around the deck."

"Ooh, now there's a thought."

Wolfgang shook his head and turned his attention to the docking of his ship.

Eric Longstaff, the second lieutenant, stood beside Richard Brazier, the fourth, and whispered something to him. Brazier grinned and shook his hand.

The men were not given shore leave so as to conceal their true numbers. No more than sixty men were on deck at any time and all the loading was done by nets. They reprovisioned for a trip to Britain and took on water and fuel. Beth went ashore to make contact with Troupial. Her notes said, when the Ventura was in dock, to go to the Pastora Church which was near the docks on a Friday evening, sit in the fourth pew from the front on the right-hand side, wearing a scarlet shawl over her hair. Troupial would meet her there.

After fifteen minutes someone sat beside her and said, "The hummingbirds only sip the sweetest nectar."

To which she answered, "But the Sugar Bandit steals it all."

"Come with me."

The two of them curtsied to the altar and crossed themselves before leaving. Two young women wearing shawls over their heads didn't draw any attention and they made their way to a house not far away. Once inside, Troupial removed her shawl to reveal a very pretty dark-haired Spanish girl with dark brown eyes.

"You are Chaton?"

"I am but you cannot call me that in public. I need a Spanish name." She dropped her shawl to her shoulders.

"With that hair we should call you La Zorra."

"That's funny. My great, times six, grandmother was called that by the inquisition. They didn't mean it in a respectful way."

"Well, I will call you Rosa, I am Manuela. How did your grandmother upset the inquisition?"

"They killed her lover, so she spent several years burning Jesuit priests until she found the one responsible. She killed him by hanging him in a gibbet from the bowsprit of her ship."

Manuela shuddered.

"We have identified several shipping agents here who seem to have had an unusual number of their ships attacked by pirates."

Beth walked to the door and nodded to someone outside. Manuela stiffened and her hand went to the butt of a pistol hidden in her sash. A man walked in, older than Beth, grey hair salted his temples and above his ears, but he was obviously very fit and stood erect.

"This is Garai, he is a special agent and a specialist in breaking into buildings and investigating. He will assist you until I return."

"You are going somewhere?" Manuela said.

"I will be away for a couple of weeks. I have something that needs to be finished."

Loading and replenishing finished, the Venturer prepared to leave port. Several suspected watchers had been identified and three had been followed back to the schooners. Another two were followed to the offices of shipping agents. Whether they were part of the privateering community or not was yet to be seen.

They left harbour, warping out into open water before setting sail. Wolfgang set a course that would take advantage of the gulf current that circulated clockwise around the gulf. This was normal practice for merchantmen as it was quicker than trying to sail across it. They had almost put Veracruz under the horizon when the lookout called, "Deck there, them two schooners have left port and are following."

"As expected," Wolfgang said to Beth who was on the quarterdeck. "Mr McGivern, you may resume running this ship navy style."

"Aye, aye, Sir!" McGivern said.

"He's certainly happy about that," Beth said.

"Sailing like a merchantman offends his sense of correctness."

"Where do you think they will spring the trap?"

"Where we have least room for manoeuvre, probably between the Bahamas and Florida."

Beth looked thoughtful. "Could we capture one of those schooners intact?"

"Probably if we let them get up beside us."

"I think we could use one."

Beth went to her cabin as they sailed up the Florida Keys and opened her trunk. At the bottom was an outfit she had made in England. She put on the bodice and Sandra pulled the laces tight before tying them off. She slipped on tight-fitting, buckskin trousers and buckled a broad-tooled leather belt around her waist from which she hung her small sword and main gauche. Her pistols were slipped into holsters on cross belts.

When she arrived on deck carrying her rifle, the officers stopped with their jaws dropped. "Lord above, would you look at her!" Midshipman Stirling gawped, earning him a clip around the ear from McGivern.

"Mind your manners, boy."

Wolfgang looked her up and down. "Just like your mother," he muttered.

"I heard the lookout say that the schooners are closing in. I thought I should be ready," Beth said.

The trousers offered protection but made her curves obvious, the leather bodice likewise. Knee-high leather boots with ridged soles to provide grip on a slippery deck finished the ensemble. She was dressed for war and the Caribbean hadn't seen her like for two hundred years.

The schooners were indeed closing in slowly. The cargo of cochineal too valuable to ignore and anyway they had orders from England.

"The Mermaid and Griffon should be waiting to cut her off," Captain Trent of the Genevieve said to his first mate.

"Aye, we will have her well and truly surrounded. The Mermaid will position across her bow. Us and the Griffon either side to board and the Spirit will cross her stern."

"Two ships approaching from ahead," the lookout cried.

"They have timed their approach perfectly," McGivern commented.

"Aye they have. Bring the ship to quarters, load all guns with chain, I want to disable them as soon as possible once they engage. Then sink all of them except that one." He pointed to the one sailing wide to come up on their port side.

Wolfgang had previously ordered their rigging fitted with preventer stays and chains on the spars. The pirates would go for his rigging rather than risk damaging the cargo.

It was a tense wait. Beth sat with her back against the gunnel, out of sight of the encircling ships. The gun crews were similarly hidden.

"They are signalling that we should stop," Midshipman Hepworth said.

"Spill our wind, everyone be ready."

The courses were loosed, and the wind spilled from the mains. The ship slowed. The schooners got into position with the ones either side, closing to board. Wolfgang waited until they were just fifty yards away.

"Run out and fire as you bear! Run up our colours"

The men flew to their tasks, topmen hauled up the mains, gun ports flew open, and the big eighteens were rolled out. On the afterdeck the covers were ripped off the carronades and on the fore the hut collapsed revealing the two huge sixty-four-pound carronades. Below decks the eighteen-pound stern chasers ran out of the transom. Supplemented by two thirty-six-pound carronades at the stern on the quarterdeck.

Smoke and flame erupted from all sides of the ship, and she shuddered with the recoil. Chain howled across the water, slashing rigging and shattering fragile masts. The pirates were caught completely by surprise. The captain of the Griffin was about to order his men to open fire when a bullet took him through the throat.

"Nice shot," Wolfgang complemented Beth as she swiftly reloaded the Hall 1819 rifle. It had a swivel breach that opened to facilitate rapid loading.

Beth didn't answer, just closed the breach and brought the rifle up ready to fire again. This time she chose an officer who was commanding the guns. She took a breath and waited for the roll.

"Got him," she said as he fell to the deck.

The main guns on that side fired into the rigging again disabling the schooner and leaving her wallowing. The other three were not so lucky. The starboard guns had reloaded with canister over ball and blasted their schooner between wind and water. Their third broadside (in less than one and a half minutes from the first) was ball and was aimed at the waterline.

The forward carronades were reloaded with small ball. Four-pound cricket-ball-sized lumps of iron. They smashed everything at main deck height. They reloaded with smashers and shot the hull out at water level.

At the stern the chasers and carronades raked the schooners rigging fore to aft, then lowered their sights and smashed her bow. They reloaded and let her have it again. She was going down.

"It's going swimmingly," Beth said as she picked off one of the few men left standing after the carronades had swept the deck of the port schooner.

"Leave a few officers for us to capture and interrogate," Wolfgang said.

Beth shifted her aim and shot a gun captain instead.

With the other three schooners sinking or drifting as useless hulks, Wolfgang ordered the helm to get them alongside the one he wanted to capture.

"Borders ready!"

The Venturer ground up alongside the Griffon and grapnels were fired across from swivel guns.

"Boarders away!"

It wasn't much of a fight. The pirates were more inclined to surrender than put up any resistance and their colours were brought down.

"I suppose you want this ship for yourself," Wolfgang said as he and Beth walked the Griffins deck.

"Oh, thank you, Uncle Wolfgang, that is so nice of you," Beth beamed at him. "Did I surprise you with my outfit?"

Wolfgang remembered his rash statement from earlier. "Not at all," he said and walked away.

Richard Brazier passed a coin to Eric Longstaff who flipped it and caught it before slipping it into his waistcoat pocket.

"Mr Brazier!" Wolfgang roared.

"Sir?"

"I want this ship repaired and sixty men for crew. You will stay as senior officer. Miss Bethany will be in overall command as the resident senior agent. This ship is now an official part of the Flotilla on active duty in the gulf. Get the prisoners aboard the Unicorn. We are going back to England."

"Rename the ship the Fox," Beth said. "I will make up papers to say we are American out of Charleston."

The damaged mainmast was replaced, using a mast salvaged from one of the hulks before it was sunk, and her rigging repaired. The decks were scrubbed clean. Shot damage was repaired and repainted. By the time the Unicorn left, the Fox was as good as new.

"Captain Brazier, would you be so kind as to set sail for Veracruz."

"Aye, aye, M'aam."

"And do not be too navy, we are American privateers."

Richard shouted the orders; he had Midshipman Stephen Donaldson as his first mate who ran to execute them. This was his first command, and he was loving it.

Beth sat in the cabin and created a set of fake papers for the ship. Her forging skills weren't really tested as the official documents were easy to replicate as was a letter of marque.

She put the ship's owner as Miss Rosa Collins of Charleston, South Carolina.

When she had finished and the papers were lying on her desk drying, she reflected that Scarlett would have been proud of her. Now she could use the Fox to infiltrate and disrupt the privateers. At the sound of hammering from above she smiled at the final leaving present Wolfgang had left her, a pair of shiny new carronades which were being mounted on pivot carriages at that very moment. She turned to the papers they had discovered aboard. The most important to the prosecution of Elfrid James had been taken by Wolfgang. But she still had some interesting ones to go through.

It appeared that the privateers would offload their ill begotten goods in Cuba along with any hulls worth selling. She would have to look into that. She also found a box of coins hidden in a space under the floor covered by a trapdoor and rug. Wolfgang's men had found similar caches in the hulks. She counted the coins into piles by denomination and value then added the total up. Five hundred, thirty-two and a half reals. That would fund her endeavours nicely.

The holds on the ship were only a fraction full. They had obviously been counting on filling them from the Venturer. She found it funny that in spite of the success the name change had given them, Wolfgang couldn't wait to have her proper name back on the stern.

There was a knock on the door.

"Come in."

Richard entered. "Miss Beth,"

"Rosa,"

"Sorry. Miss Rosa, can I ask what you will be using the Fox for?"

"We will be attacking privateers. Why?"

"Well, if we are getting into a fight, we will need more men. Sixty is a good-sized crew for this ship for general sailing and defending ourselves. But if we are going to take on a privateer, we will need another forty odd."

"Hmm, we need to recruit then." She got up and pulled a chart from the rack. "Where are we on here?"

"Just off the Bahamas, here." He pointed to their position.

"What route will we take back to Veracruz?"

"Along the north coast of Cuba, then down between Cuba and Dominica and past Jamaica to the north, past the Cayman Islands and into the gulf. That way we have the current on our stern the whole way."

"So, we could easily put into Jamaica."

"Yes, we could, but why?"

"We need more men, we will find some there."

"But we are navy."

"No, we are a privateer, and they will be signed on to sail on a privateer. For the moment the crew needs to think and act like privateers. I'm sure they can manage."

Beth heard the call of "Land Hoe!" from the mainmast lookout and went up on deck. As the Fox was flush decked, the quarterdeck was denoted by an imaginary line rather than anything physical. She was dressed in her fighting clothes and stood beside Richard who did his very best to keep his eyes forward. The problem was he was only a year or two older than her and was extremely attracted to her.

Jamaica appeared on the horizon dead ahead and they steered for Kingston Harbour. They slipped in past what was left of Port Royal after the 1692 earthquake and entered the bay. There was a Royal Naval hospital on the peninsula and that gave her an idea. She took her letter of authority from the strong box and asked Richard to accompany her with his commission.

Once they had anchored, a crew rowed them to the landing by the newly (1818) rebuilt hospital. Beth and Richard went ashore and asked where the commanding officer was. They were directed to a cottage nearby. Richard knocked on the door and it was answered by a servant.

"We are here to see the commander," he said.

"Who should I say is visiting?"

"Captain Brazier and…" he looked at Beth questioningly.

"Chaton," she said with a smile.

The servant looked her up and down, surprised at her dress.

"Well go on, announce us," she chided.

The commander was a navy captain surgeon and grumpy at having his siesta disturbed. He looked over half-moon glasses at them and said, quite abruptly, "Good gad gall, what kind of outfit is that?"

Richard doffed his hat.

"And you are out of uniform, sah."

"Tush, stop being such a grump," Beth said. "We are here to take some of your excess patients away. The fit ones."

"What? On whose authority?"

Beth handed him the letter and Richard handed him his commission and orders. He read both, going redder by the minute.

"I've never heard of such a thing. This is signed by the foreign secretary," he said holding up Beth's letter.

"And countersigned by the secretary to the First Lord. It clearly instructs any naval officer, whatever the rank, to assist me on request. Captain Brazier is in command of the Fox, and we need more crew."

"I will have to talk to the admiral."

"It will not make a shred of difference; I need crew and I am asking you for them."

He blustered for a minute then realised it was hopeless. The extraordinary young woman in front of him just stood one hand on her sword and the other on her hip. He suddenly remembered something.

"You work for Admiral Turner?"

"I do."

He grunted something under his breath then called, "HECTOR!"

Hector was an administrator.

"How many patients have we got who are about to be discharged?"

"Twelve imminently and another four in the next week."

"Are they all fit to crew a ship?"

"Some need to be on light duties for a while to build up their strength but in general they are all fit." He stopped and referred to a book he carried. "No, that's not quite true. There are two with hernias that are being discharged."

"So how many can start now?" Richard said.

"Now? Eleven."

"And in a week?"

"Three."

"I will take all fourteen, the ones that were to be discharged in a week will be allowed to rest for another week onboard."

The commander nodded.

"I will prepare the papers. Which ship?"

"The Fox."

Three hours after Beth and Richard got back to the Fox the lookout called, "Boat ahoy!"

"Admiral's flag lieutenant," the cox called back.

"Come alongside."

The flag lieutenant and six marines came up the side. They were met by Richard, Sergeant Bright and his twelve marines. All in civilian dress of course and armed with Baker rifles.

"Are you Captain Brazier?" the lieutenant said with a very upper-class nasally accent.

"I am."

"You are under arrest, by order of the admiral."

There was a series of clicks as hammers were pulled to full cock and one very close to his ear.

"Really? Would you like to rephrase that?" a very soft female voice said.

He turned slowly and found himself looking down the barrels of an unusual but quite large bore pistol. Close behind it was a pair of grey/green eyes framed in auburn hair. They didn't blink.

He looked to his marines that were stood very still under the cocked rifles of the men who had met them.

"Sergeant Bright, please have your marines stand down. I have this," she said.

"Yes, Ma'am. At ease."

"Now, shall we proceed in a more civilised and mannerly way?" Beth said.

"Um, the admiral, Sir Charles Rowley, requests the pleasure of your company."

"There that's much nicer." Beth smiled and stepped away, holstering the pistol after putting the hammer in its safe position.

"I need to change, be back in a minute. You two get to know each other." She walked to the stair that led to her cabin. The lieutenant's eyes never left her backside.

She dressed in a light summer dress and put her pistols in garter holsters on her thighs. A summer hat with a broad brim finished the ensemble held on with hat pins that were more like stilettos.

"Shall we go?" she said as they came up on deck.

The two lieutenants smiled at the sight of her although the flag was slightly disappointed at not seeing the admiral's reaction to the leathers.

Once in the boat the flag introduced himself, "Reginald Percival-Simms at your service."

"Chaton."

"Chaton? Kitten?"

"You speak French, how nice."

The rest of the trip was in silence, except the officer of marines who asked Richard, "Was that Sergeant Bright of the marines?"

"Yes, it was."

"Then those men were all marines?"

"Yes, they are."

"Oh." He lapsed into silence as well.

They came alongside the flagship, a three decked, one hundred-and-ten-gun, first rate. "I will call for a chair."

"No need," Beth said and used a hidden ribbon to lift the hem of her skirt and hold it out of the way as she shinnied up the battens.

"Is she always like this?" Simms asked Richard."

"You do not know the half of it," he said with a grin.

They were escorted to the admiral's cabin. The bellow that bade them enter testified to his mood.

Beth stepped in and decided that a purely business-like approach would be best.

"Admiral, if you would be so kind to read this," she said without a word of greeting and handed him her letter.

"What?" he said, taking it without thinking.

"I think I was perfectly clear. Please read the letter. We will get along a lot better after you have."

He glared at her and scanned the letter, blinked twice then he read it again and took it to the window to examine the seal and the signature.

"I can only assume you are one of Canning's people."

"Correct."

"What are you doing stealing my men?"

"I need them."

"Why?"

"That is confidential."

He sat with a huff and scanned the letter again.

"You are Chaton?"

"You can call me that."

"Phillips! Coffee for three. Lieutenant, you are dismissed. You two please sit down."

Once the lieutenant had left, the admiral settled down and waited for the coffee to be delivered. When it had been served, he said, "You are an agent for the Intelligence Service?"

"I am."

"God you lot get younger. The Fox is not a navy ship."

"It is part of the Special Operations Flotilla of the overseas department."

"You are navy," he said to Richard.

"Lieutenant Richard Brazier, Sir."

"So, I gather. I checked you on the list. According to that you appear to be at sea in a ship called HMS Silent."

"A necessary fiction, Sir."

The admiral shook his head, obviously not happy.

"How many men do you have on the Fox?"

"Sixty, Sir."

"And she flies an American flag."

"A rus de guerre, Sir."

"Who are we at war with that no one told me about?"

"Confidential information, I'm afraid, Admiral," Beth said.

"You damn spies—"

"Agents, please," Beth interrupted with a sweet smile.

"You damn agents and your secrets." He turned back to Richard.

"How many men do you need?"

"A complement of one hundred would be ideal. We are forty men short."

"I can give you twenty. Can you get the rest from shore?"

"Thank you, I believe we can," Beth said, secretly thinking the admiral would use this opportunity to get rid of his troublemakers. Well, she would tame them.

While Richard was busy recruiting, Beth took a trip to their newly acquired plantation. Malakai had installed a new manager and Beth met him at the house.

"Bertram Barkley, Miss Bethany."

"I have seen your resumé; you are very experienced."

"Malakai made me an offer I couldn't refuse. My previous employer was none too pleased."

"His loss is our gain, welcome to The Den."

"The Den?"

"Yes, this plantation was called that when it was owned by my ancestor Scarlett Browning and I want the name to be re-initiated."

"You are an ancestor of that pirate?"

"You know of her?"

"She is legendary on the island. As famous as Morgan and the later pirates. I didn't know she owned this estate."

"Not only owned but founded it."

She had afternoon tea then went out to meet the workers. They were delighted she was back. On a whim she asked that they tattoo the iguana on her wrist. An old woman, the same one she had met before, came forward with a stick with a thorn pushed through the end and a pot of ink. Beth gritted her teeth.

Before she left, her wrist bandaged, she asked Bertram to accompany her to the cellar.

"There should be a door here to another room, can you get it opened?"

He left and came back with two men with hammers. They went to work, sweating even in the coolness of the cellar. They soon discovered that the door had simply been plastered over and they had it exposed in short order.

Beth tried the handle. It was locked. She examined the lock. It was large, strong but simple. She delved into her purse and came out with a boot hook and added one of the pins from her hair. The lock resisted but she finally got it to move. She opened the door and it stuck so she gave way to the two men and they used their shoulders to push it open.

Dry air washed out of the open doorway making their lamps flicker. Beth waited until the air stilled, then, carrying a lamp before her, stepped inside.

"Oh, my lord. They never left."

There, side by side, were two old coffins. Brass plaques named them as Stephen and Scarlett Browning. Beth stood over Scarlett's and felt a warm touch. She looked around, she was quite alone, the others staying outside out of respect.

"Well, Grandmother, we are back," she said.

The Fox picked her up at Annotto Bay. The crypt had been sealed with a new lock which only she had the key to. Her wrist had healed nicely, and the tattoo could be discreetly hidden. They had a full crew, now it was time to get to work.

Veracruz

The Fox, now totally unrecognisable as the Griffon, anchored in the harbour rather than tied up. That was because the men that the admiral had sent her had turned out to be a bunch of sea lawyers and deserters. She had had to impress them that she was capable of being in charge by slicing up one, he was alive but would take time to heal properly and feeding another to the sharks. Which left her two men short, and she was annoyed.

A boat took her ashore. She took Sandra with her so as not to leave her with the temptation to tease the men. She assumed her cover identity before they left and dressed Sandra like a serving girl. Manuela was waiting for them.

"You have a different ship."

"You were watching?"

"I have men watching the harbour at all times. What happened with the English schooners?"

"One of them is out there, the rest are at the bottom of the sea."

"And your ship? The Venturer?"

"Hardly a scratch and only four men wounded."

"My god! I would have liked to have been there."

"To be honest it was all over as soon as the Venturer opened fire. You see she is really a British heavy frigate with forty-four eighteen-pounders and a load of carronades. They didn't stand a chance."

"We now need to find out who else is supplying information to the privateers here and in other ports in Columbia and Venezuela."

"What will you do then? We have no jurisdiction here and the magistrates are not likely to prosecute one of their own."

"We will deal with the problem ourselves. What has Garai discovered?"

"He will be back soon from watching one of the agents. He has been going out late at night to enter the agent's premises."

Garai returned on time and sat down to brief the two of them on what he had found.

"I have men observing the shipping agents which we identified as likely sources for the privateers. I have searched their premises. Only one showed up evidence of the agent being the source himself. Of the rest our surveillance and the search has shown up that two have clerks that might be the source. The last, we think is innocent."

Manuela chipped in, "My men have been monitoring the docks and we have noticed men watching what ships are loaded with what. We followed several and found that some were just rumour mongers or informants but four were reporting directly to agents."

"That could be the agents checking that they were not being stiffed by the captains," Beth said.

"True, so we checked which ships were being watched against the agents dealing with them."

"And?"

"Two in particular were taking an unhealthy interest in high-value cargos that were not being handled by their agents."

Garai placed two fliers on the table that advertised shipping agents. "These are the two in question."

Beth picked them up.

"Carlos Jimenez and Pedro Ramirez. I assume you searched their offices."

"Yes, they were two of the ones I searched. I did two others for comparison."

That was sound practice. Establish the norm and look for exceptions.

"Let's have a chat with the clerk who you think is collaborating and see what we can get out of him. But before that I want to search his home." She thought about it for a moment or two then added, "Let's see if he has a family, that might give us all the leverage we need."

That night after midnight when all the lanterns had been doused in the house of Miguel Dias, two shadowy figures dressed in black and hooded, slipped through an open window. The house was in a nice street and was probably better than you would expect a humble clerk to own. They methodically searched the ground floor, then moved upstairs. They moved carefully, testing each step before putting weight on the foot so not a floorboard creaked.

The first room had a baby in a cot. The slimmer of the two reached in and gently picked it up. It was held gently and slept on soundly. They moved to the main bedroom. There, fast asleep, was Miguel and his wife.

The larger of the two intruders pulled a knife. A nastily curved one that glinted wickedly in the moonlight coming through the window. He sat on the bed beside Miguel and placed a hand over the man's mouth while the knife rested against his throat. The other, still carrying the baby, sat beside his wife.

Miguel woke and went to sit up but froze as the hand restrained him and the knife tickled his throat.

"Shh, Miguel, don't wake the baby."

His eyes swivelled, the whites showing, he could see his son being held by the second intruder, he nodded.

"Good, you understand." The voice coming from under the hood was husky and had a slight accent. The hand was removed.

"I am going to ask you some questions. You can answer yes or no by nodding or shaking your head."

"Are you selling information about ships and their cargo to the privateers? Oh, before you answer, please bear in mind we have your son."

His face twisted in anguish, then he nodded.

"Excellent. Does your employer know?"

He shook his head, carefully as the knife was still there.

"Are you targeting English ships?"

Again, a shake of the head.

"But you do give the details of English ships as well as Spanish and other nations."

He nodded; eyes still wide.

His wife stirred and the other figure reached out a hand. She muttered in her sleep and settled, snoring gently. The figure relaxed.

"From now on you will not pass on the details of English ships but you will pass on these details." He placed a sheet of paper by his head. "Remember we know where you live."

The two stood and the baby was placed on the bed between them. They left as quietly as they had come. Miguel watched them go then a sob escaped his lips. The baby stirred and his wife woke. "Miguel? Why is the baby here?" she said sleepily.

"He was fretting so I brought him in with us."

"Put him back in his cot," she said and went back to sleep.

Manuel lay awake for a long time.

The paper gave him the name of a ship, the Fox, and a cargo of hardwoods and personal goods. The personal goods were most interesting because that usually meant bullion.

"He passed information to a Columbian captain this morning," Manuela reported.

"Perfect," Beth said to Garai. "Come on, the Fox needs to be loaded to close the trap."

The loading concluded with a large, obviously heavy, chest being carried aboard, and a blatant bribe made to a customs official. The money disappeared into his jacket, and he left the dock whistling a happy tune.

One of the snitches left the docks and went straight to a local bar where he met the Columbian captain. Coins were paid and information transferred. The captain went to his ship.

The Fox left port, at no time had more than thirty men been visible. She sailed serenely past the fortress and out into the gulf. She went with the current and seemed blissfully unaware that she was being followed. Then the morning two days later they woke to find the Columbian off their port beam.

"If he gets any closer he will be boarding us," Manuela said. She had insisted on coming along to see what happened.

"Tush, they are still a cable off," Beth said and waved to them.

The two women were on deck in summer dresses and bonnets to give the ship an air of innocence.

Manuela waved as well. "How close do you want them?"

"Oh, about fifty yards."

Manuela looked aft.

"Is that a British flag that boy is holding?"

"Yes, it will be raised just before we fire. It would be a crime to start the fight under false colours." Manuela wondered at that twisted morality.

The Columbian closed the gap, raised a black flag and when they were close enough Richard shouted, "Raise our colours, run out, fire as you bear."

The gun ports shot up and the cannon rolled out. On the after deck the cover on the carronade was torn off and it belched a load of canister at the other ships wheel. That was closely followed by loads of canister over shot from the eight nine-pounders.

Beth's dress slid to the deck revealing her fighting leathers and she drew her sword and a pistol.

"Close and board!" she cried.

Manuela looked at her in amazement, and had to admit she looked bloody magnificent. The wind blew Beth's hair into an auburn mane, the leathers did nothing to hide that she was all woman.

"I have got to get me some of those!" she said.

The carronades fired again followed by the main battery at almost point-blank range. The ships ground together, and Beth leapt across to the other ship with her men. She shot a man and skewered another, kicking him off her blade. She engaged a young man who if she had time to notice was barely old enough to shave. He fell to a punch from her knuckle guard.

She had a moment's respite and swapped her pistol for her main gauche.

She spotted their captain standing on the quarterdeck surrounded by dead bodies. She walked towards him, swatting away anyone who got in her way. He saw her coming and took a stance, his rapier in his left hand and a dagger in his right.

Left-handed, well two can play that game.

She swapped hands. He looked surprised. She grinned.

"I do not fight women," he said in English.

"You will or die where you stand," Beth replied.

He shook his head then launched an attack trying to take her by surprise. He failed. Beth swatted his blade away almost contemptuously.

She counterattacked, using a two-handed style unseen outside of Spain for a hundred years. He was the one to be surprised this time. Beth attacked with both hands forcing him to work very hard to defend himself.

She stepped back and saluted him with her blade. He had survived so far. He saluted back and immediately attacked as he brought his blade down. Beth carefully backed up making sure she didn't trip over a corpse or slip on blood. Parrying with her sword, she pretended to slip. He thrust aiming for her heart. She parried with the main gauche letting his blade slip into the arms that ran parallel along her blade from the cross guard.

She twisted.

There was a loud ping, and his blade was snapped halfway down the blade.

"Oops," Beth said, and placed the tip of her sword against his throat.

He dropped both his weapons. Beth prodded gently, "And the pistol."

The weapon hit the floor.

"Order your men to put down their weapons."

He glared at her and opened his mouth to say something, Beth didn't give him the chance. She prodded his throat hard enough to draw blood. She cocked her head to the side and raised her eyebrows expectantly.

"Put down your weapons, we have struck!" he bellowed.

Most heard it and stopped fighting, some men at the front didn't and kept going until someone either killed them or rapped them on the head from behind.

When peace was finally restored, Beth had the captain's hands tied behind his back. She was joined by Richard and Stephen.

"We are checking the holds and I have a man searching the captain's cabin for documents."

"Excellent," Beth said, and walked over to the captain.

"What is your name?"

The man spat at her feet.

"Garai, dear, would you be so kind as to throw a hook over that yard for me."

Garai grinned; he knew exactly what Beth was about to do. He went one better though and rigged a tackle and had it hung from the yard.

Beth smiled at him as he presented her with the hook he had tied on the end.

"Thank you."

She turned to the captain and slipped the hook through the bindings on his wrists.

"Now, I am going to ask you nicely to answer once. After that it is going to get very uncomfortable." She half turned away and then said, "For you but not for me."

She took the other end of the rope and stood in front of him.

"What is your name?"

He glared at her, head held high.

She pulled on the rope.

An hour later she had not just his name but the name of the ship's owner, where they sold their goods, and any number of other questions that she or Richard thought of.

"One dead, three wounded bad enough not to be able to work. What are we going to do with the prisoners?" Richard said as the two met in her cabin. Beth had an idea, well rather she remembered something her great grandmother used to do.

"Come with me."

The Isabella was still tied up alongside. The remains of her crew sat on the main deck covered by two men with swivels loaded with canister. The wounded and dead were lined up on deck.

"Stand up and get into two lines."

The men shuffled into two lines. Some looked resentful, some curious.

"You cost me four men who can no longer work my ship That annoys me and when I am annoyed, I do bad things. You need to cheer me up and make me happy.

How do you do that? I hear you ask. I want two men to replace each of those I have lost. In case you cannot multiply four by two, I need eight men."

"What if we don't?" a swarthy individual asked.

Beth walked over to the wounded and walked down the line. She came to one that had recently expired. She pulled her pistol and shot the corpse in the head. The men didn't know the man was already dead and recoiled. Beth didn't say anymore, just walked back to stand in front of them and waited while turning the second barrel into line.

A good-looking man with a goatee stepped forward. "I would be interested to crew for such a captain."

Beth took a half-real from Richard and tossed it to him. He snatched it out of the air. He was now hers. He was followed by another half dozen and then by four more.

"Put the rest ashore somewhere remote," Beth ordered. "The captain stays here."

Yucatan was the chosen spot to drop them then they headed to Havana. The ship and the cargo of maize it already carried should sell for a fair price.

While they sailed, Beth wrote an extended sea letter to Sebastian telling him how much she missed him and what she was doing. Some of it was encrypted in their private code. She didn't want just anybody to be able to read it. She also wrote to her mother, father and siblings. Her report to Admiral Turner was done last and, as they taught her at the academy it was concise and to the point with no embellishment.

The prisoners didn't like being dumped on the northern shore of the Yucatan and protested mightily. Beth put an end to all that nonsense by shooting one in the arm. After that they went meekly. Somehow, she seemed to unnerve them.

Havana

The entered Havana Bay past the looming fortresses that protected the entrance. What surprised them was there were other fortresses covering the bay itself. The pilot, a pock-marked, goatee-bearded sour-faced, son of a bitch, had them moor to a buoy.

"You will be allowed to dock only when you have a customer for your goods." He left without a 'by your leave' or 'thank you'.

Beth called Richard to her, "You, Garai and I will go ashore and find someone who will buy our goods."

"I'll get a boat around."

Richard called orders and the jolly boat was brought alongside, a cox and crew allocated.

"Boss, may I have a word?" It was Carlos the first man to volunteer from the Isabella.

"Yes. What is it?"

"I heard that the skipper was going with you to find a merchant."

"What of it?" Beth wondered where he was going with this.

"I have been here many times and I know most of the merchants and a couple of good men who could use the hull." He looked like he wanted to say more but was uncertain what the reception would be.

"And?"

"I am volunteering to go with you to help you."

"Why? We stole your ship."

"I was with them for the money. You took them easily. Your skipper is better than that jumped-up first mate that we had. Your crew is better as well."

"What is your rating?"

"On here I am a topman, but I was a boatswain on the Isabella."

Richard returned, "Boats ready when you are." As usual he spoke English.

"Who is the cox?"

"Davidson."

"Carlos here is rated bosun."

"I know, but I don't have a vacancy."

"I need a cox."

"You never said." Richard realised he'd made a mistake as soon as he said it as Beth's eyes turned grey. "I mean, you should. You need someone to cover your back beside Garai."

She gave him a slow look.

"He will replace Davidson in the boat and will be my personal cox from now on."

Carlos looked on curiously; he had never sailed on a ship where the owner was on board, they usually preferred to stay in the shadows. Not only was the owner here but she was a fascinating woman as well as surprisingly young. They were talking in English, which meant he had no clue what was being said but he did recognise the moment when the skipper said something he shouldn't.

"You will cox the boat ashore and come with us. If you try anything I will shoot you."

He had no doubt she would.

They tied up at a wooden dock and Beth, Richard, Garai, and Carlos went ashore. The crew would wait. Beth gave the most senior crewman enough money to buy them all some bread, cheese and beer.

"There is a merchant that specialises in grain and foods that will take the maize. There are two that trade in hardwoods. Do you want to sell your bullion?"

"What bullion?"

"In the large chest?"

"Oh that!" Beth laughed, "That was just bricks."

"Bricks?"

"Bricks," Garai said, giving him a dangerous look.

"Ay Caramba! We lost the ship for a chest of bricks? Santa Maria! You are a devil woman."

Richard asked Garai to translate, then burst out laughing. Soon they were all in tears as they laughed, sobering only for someone to say "bricks" and set them all off again.

Carlos was as good as his word and got them good prices for their cargo and an unexpectedly large one for the hull. The owner got a quarter, and the captain got a quarter, the mates/warrants got an eighth between them as there were only six of them, and the rest was divided equally amongst the crew. It was a tidy sum even after the deduction for the social fund, and they had a very happy ship.

Beth had lookouts noting the names of any ships that looked like privateers that came in and gave the crew shore leave. They were soon spending their ill-gotten gains on rum and women. Beth and her officers, including Garai, had a much more sedate meal in a restaurant frequented by the upper classes.

Halfway through the meal a man approached. He looked angry.

"You!" he shouted from some ten yards away.

Beth ignored him and carried on eating the lobster she had ordered. It was delicious, served with garlic butter and salad.

"I said you, ginger bitch." He used the phrase 'Perra jengibre' which could also translate to 'ginger slut'.

Garai and Richard sat back making sure they were not in between them. Stephen went as far as to move his chair.

"What did you call me?"

"Ginger bitch, you stole one of my ships. I just saw it in the yard."

"You could always buy it back." Beth was surpassingly calm but anyone who knew her could see the warning signs. The fact that she was calm, the grey coldness in her eyes, the hand that had disappeared into a hidden pocket in her dress.

"I want compensation!"

"You should ask your captain for that. He was incompetent."

"He is my brother! What have you done with him?"

Beth laughed a cold laugh.

"He is well and, in my brig, you can have him back for," she made a show of thinking about it, "ten thousand reals."

"What? Why don't I just kill you here and now." He started to raise a pistol and suddenly found himself looking down the barrels of four of them.

Beth made a show of dabbing her lips with a napkin then stood. She still had her pistol in her hand but kept it at her side as she walked up to him.

"You have disturbed my dinner and called me ginger, and added to that you called me a slut. The first two are enough to get you killed and the third I don't give a shit about. So, we will settle this like civilised people, despite your obvious lack of breeding. I will meet you at dawn tomorrow on the docks in front of the ropewalk. There we will settle the issue with swords." She turned and walked back towards the table but stopped halfway. "Don't forget the ten thousand reals to pay for your brother after you lose," she said over her shoulder.

The next morning Beth, dressed in her leather trousers and a white silk blouse, waited patiently on the dock for her opponent to arrive. Seconds had arrived at the restaurant to make the arrangements before they finished their meal. She carried a sheathed rapier with a basket hilt. It had a forty-inch blade and was made from Toledo steel by the same master bladesmith that made her mother's sword. The basket hilt was engraved and highlighted in gold; the pommel capped with the Stockley family arms. Engraved in Latin below the ricasso was *Virtus Fortitudo Integritas,* Virtue, Strength, Integrity.

Beth unclipped the sheath and drew the sword. It glinted wickedly in the dawn sun as she practised a few loosening exercises. A carriage pulled up and several men got out. She heard Garai and Richard step up behind her.

Her opponent stepped out in front of his seconds, and one took his cloak from his shoulders. He was dressed in a white shirt with a frilled front. He too had a rapier but his was of a plain workman like variety. That didn't make it any less dangerous. It had a forty-inch blade and looked to be razor sharp.

The seconds came together and talked. Richard shook his head as he returned, indicating that the challenged would not apologise. Beth didn't care, she was looking forward to this. She stepped forward and raised her blade in salute then took her stance waiting for him to come forward.

She watched his eyes as he advanced and knew what he was about to do. Instead of taking his guard he launched an attack without warning. Beth performed a perfect circular parry which left her with the opportunity to counterattack. She flicked her blade toward his nose forcing him to make a rapid and unbalancing duck. She stepped past him and slapped his ass with the flat of her blade.

"Naughty boy, that's not in the rules."

By the time he turned she was back in her ready position.

"Shall we start again?" She lowered her blade to the traditional en garde position.

He glared at her and took his guard.

"Engage!" Richard called.

She tapped his tip. He stepped to the side trying to get to her left side. Beth obliged him by stepping to her right, her footwork precise, balanced and secure. As she stepped, he attacked high, flicking his sword at her face trying to catch her off balance. Her parry sent his blade high, and her riposte put a cut in his shirt forcing him to step back. She pressed her advantage.

Juan Montego Rodriguez parried frantically as she forced him backwards. He had never experienced such speed before. Her well-balanced blade was an extension of her wrist which was surprisingly strong. He knew she could have scored on him a number of times but just chose to slit his shirt. That warned him that she had absolute control. He had never met a man with this level of skill, let alone a woman.

She broke off her attack for the second time and took her guard.

"Do you want to apologise yet?" she said.

He was growing tired and desperate.

"No," he replied and charged her hoping to catch her unawares.

She pirouetted like a ballet dancer, her hair swirling around her head. Her sword sliced.

Juan staggered to a stop. His sword held limply in his hand. For some reason his fingers didn't have any strength. He was aware that his seconds were rushing to his side. The sword fell from his nerveless fingers clattering to the ground. A rivulet of blood ran down his thumb and to the ground. His gaze followed it back up to his forearm where his shirt was red with blood. He swooned.

Beth wiped her blade with a rag given to her by Garai. She retrieved her sheath and slid the blade home before clipping it to her belt. Richard walked over from where he had attended the dressing of her opponent's wound. His forearm had been sliced to the bone and the tendons severed. A good surgeon might save it and the use of his hand.

"Did he bring the ransom for the captain?"

"He is unconscious, you almost severed his arm. There was a cut mark in the bone."

"You could see it? Maybe I hit a little hard."

"He might lose it."

"Hard luck that." She wasn't at all sorry.

"Madam," one of his seconds approached, "Senor Rodrigues wishes to speak to you."

Beth followed him to their coach and found him sat inside looking very pale. She stood in the doorway.

"Madam Rosa, I concede the win to you. I am unfortunately unable to continue."

Beth nodded.

"My brother."

"The price hasn't changed."

Rodrigues sighed and flicked his left hand to one of his seconds who took a small chest out of the coach and handed it to her.

"One thousand two hundred and fifty pieces of eight. Your ten thousand reals blood money."

Beth took the chest and handed it to Garai, she turned to leave.

"What did you do with the crew?" Rodrigues asked.

"Those that didn't join my crew, I put ashore near the fishing village of Cancun in the Yucatan."

"You have some mercy then."

"I am merciful but not forgiving. I could easily have killed you, but I let you live. If we cross swords again, I will kill you without hesitation."

The three of them walked away and didn't look back so didn't see Carlos approach the coach and get in the far door. He was inside for three minutes and left in a hurry. He was back at the boat before Beth and the two others joined it to go back to the Fox.

Their work in Havana wasn't finished, Beth, Manuela and Garai worked the bars along the docks listening for rumours and gathering intelligence. Sailors when they are drunk are a boastful species and their tales of daring, exaggerated of course, all had a grain of information and truth in them. The trick was winnowing the chaff from the grain.

They went ashore dressed like locals. Beth liked the colourful dresses the girls wore and the sassy way they behaved. She took note of what they did and the effect it had on the men. She used every trick she observed, and the sailors were putty in her hands. The information was recorded and indexed. Once they set sail Beth would analyse it and decide what to do next.

It was time to go back to Veracruz. They had spent two weeks in Havana and Beth needed to send her report back to Turner. There were no British ships in port, so she decided to revisit Jamaica and send it on the navy packet. Her internal justification was that they would be passing the island anyway.

They rounded up the crew and set out. As her cox, Carlos had fairly free access to her cabin, but made sure he knocked and waited for permission before he entered. Beth had the intelligence they had gathered, and a chart laid out on her desk. She was meticulously marking routes and positions where ships had been attacked. They had already learned that there were at least two gangs operating out of Cuba in small ships that attacked almost any ship that was spotted passing between Cuba and Miami. That was having the effect that the merchant skippers were hugging the American side and risking the reefs and rocks that lined the coast.

She concluded that she couldn't do anything about Cuba apart from recommending that the British and Americans increase their patrols through the straits. What she was concentrating on were the ships leaving the major ports and being attacked by the privateers out of South America.

There was a knock at the door. She folded the chart and put it away, along with her report, in the drawer of her desk. Carlos entered all smiles.

"We are about to pass between Cuba and Dominica."

"What do you know about the privateers out of Colombia and Venezuela?"

"Not much, we worked out of Mexico. I know they call Cartagena, Barranquilla, and Caracas home as I've met some in bars."

"So did I and I got the same information."

"Why are you interested in them? You can base yourself anywhere and take ships as you find them."

"I always like to know who the opposition are and where they work from," Beth lied easily.

Carlos nodded, "Yes, then you can avoid them."

Not quite what I intend. "Yes, exactly."

Jamaica came up on the horizon just in time as a tropical storm was coming up from the southeast. It was the hurricane season and by all rights they should be tucked up safely in port. They got behind the shelter of Port Royal just as it hit and dropped two bow and a stern anchor to hold them. They couldn't even go ashore as the bay was too rough to row in. The wind veered and Richard ordered the stern anchor to be buoyed and cut away to allow the ship to swing into it.

"Is this a hurricane?" Beth asked as they sat in his cabin with Garai.

"Lord no," Richard replied, looking out at the white caps rushing past them. "The wind would be much harder."

"Harder than this? Sandra is laid up sick again and we are in port."

"It will pass soon. If the eye crosses us, we will get a short calm period before the back edge of it passes. We can get the two of you ashore then."

"Ship ahoy!" a lookout called from above.

They both looked out of the transom windows. A ship passed them, storm sails being furled as they tried to turn into wind.

"That's one of ours," Beth said.

"Looks like the Caroline," Garai said.

"They've got their anchor down. I think they will be fine now."

Beth watched as the elegant clipper dropped a second bow anchor and let the wind push her back a cable. Then sheets of rain obscured her.

The wind dropped as the eye of the storm passed over and they put Beth and Sandra in a boat for shore. Carlos was her cox of course and had the crew pull hard to get there before the eye passed. Beth noticed that the Caroline, if that was the ship, did the same. She got on shore and headed for an inn called The Mermaid.

She had just finished getting rooms when the door opened and in walked – her mother followed by Tabetha. Anyone watching might have thought they were seeing double. Garai grinned and Beth looked at her open mouthed.

"Mother, what?"

"Give me a hug and a kiss."

Beth hugged her fiercely, suddenly realising how much she had missed her.

"What are you doing here? Your father said you were in Mexico."

"We stopped by to send my report back to the admiral with our letters. We were in Cuba and making our way back to Veracruz."

"You can send them on the Caroline. She is faster than the packet and will be returning once they have loaded their cargo. Weather permitting of course."

Beth understood, the captain would try to get out of port and the hurricane belt between storms.

"I have rooms I can take the whole floor if you like."

"That would be nice."

Beth called the owner over and asked. He frowned.

"I have another guest on the third floor who I will have to ask if he will move."

"Tell him we will refund his rent," Beth said.

The innkeeper trotted off and Caroline raised an eyebrow.

"Not short of cash then?"

"We took a prize. It made a pretty penny."

They went to Beth's rooms and could hear the landlord talking to an annoyed guest who didn't want to move.

"Give me a moment," Beth said and went to the room. Garai followed her.

The door was open, and she stepped inside.

"Is there a problem?"

"Miss Bethany, I was—" the landlord said.

"I heard." She looked at the man who was short and fussy. "Did he tell you that we would reimburse your rent?"

"Yes, but that is not the point!" the man said belligerently, obviously on a moral high.

Garai stepped forward. He had pistols clipped to his cross belts, a cutlass on his left hip and a large dagger on his right. He glowered.

"You cannot bully me!" the man cried, sticking his chin out.

Beth sighed. The last thing she wanted was this man running to the governor crying that he had been threatened. But then again, her own reputation as Rosa of the Fox may be enhanced. She had noticed new bills of lading on the sideboard.

"Do you know who I am?" she said.

"No, and I don't give a damn."

She pulled her knife from its sheath and used it to examine her hair. "I am Captain Rosa of the Fox, a privateer. I am licensed to take certain ships on behalf of the American Government. Now sometimes I make a mistake and take a friendly ship. I am always sorry afterwards when I realise what we have done but by then it's too late for many of the crew."

She smiled her brightest smile at him.

"We do want to avoid accidents, don't we?" She walked to the dresser and picked up a bill of lading. "The Lincoln, sailing on the 18ᵗʰ. I mustn't forget that, I would hate to make a mistake."

Garai nodded. The little man looked horrified.

"All right, all right! I will move but under protest. Understood?"

As soon as he said that, several servants descended on the rooms and packed his belongings. When they were gone along with shorty, as Beth called him in her mind, they started cleaning and preparing the room.

Caroline was waiting for her when she got back, sat by a window that had rain hammering against it. She looked relaxed.

"Is that your ship I saw when we came in?"

"The Fox, yes. The Caroline is anchored a couple of cables behind it."

"The Fox?" Caroline laughed.

"What's wrong with that?" Beth asked, piqued.

"Oh nothing, it is just that it is what your great grandmother called her ship."

"I know, I read her journal. I named it in her honour as I did the new plantation. She is buried there with her husband in the cellar under the house."

"Yes, I read that in your letter. I left as soon as I got it."

"I instructed them to clear the graveyard. It was overgrown."

"There could be restless spirits there."

Beth looked at her questioningly. "Since when have you believed in ghosts?"

"There are stranger things in this world than we know. Have you felt her presence?"

Beth had to admit that she had.

"Well, there you are, there are many unexplained things in this world. I cannot deny them without proof."

Beth looked at the rain on the window. It was running down in a stream. "Will you come with me to the plantation? The roads will be washed out, but we can sail around to Annotto Bay and avoid all that."

"Of course, that is why I am here." She reached into her bag and pulled out a beautiful gold and emerald necklace and bracelet. "These were Scarlett's. I want to let her know we still have them."

A week later the Fox left Kingston and sailed around the island to Annotto Bay. From there it was a short walk to the plantation. They were greeted by Bertram who hid his surprise well. Rooms were organised then Beth took her mother down into the cellar.

The door to what was now a crypt had been restored to its former glory and a new lock fitted. Beth had the key and let them in. Caroline sighed as she saw the coffins and ran her hand over the brass plaques. She took out the jewels and laid them on Scarlett's coffin.

They both felt it. A wave of love and pride.

"Grandmother," Caroline said with tears in her eyes as she and hugged Beth.

Author's Notes

Quinggong – A forerunner of f ree running and Parkour. Translated it means Lightness Skill.

Portland Street in 1820 is now known as Regent Street.

Flibbertigibbet – a gossip or chatterbox

Fencing terms used in this book:

Compound attack

Also composed attack. An attack or riposte incorporating one or more feints to the opposite line that the action finishes in. Compound attacks are usually used to draw multiple reactions from an opponent, or against an opponent who uses complex parries.

Croisé

(Archaic) also cross, semi-bind; an action in which one fencer forces the opponent's blade into the high or low line on the same side, by taking it with the guard and forte of their own blade.

Disengage

A type of feint. Disengages are usually executed in conjunction with an extension/attack, though technically, they are just a deception around the opponent's blade. To use in an attack, feint an attack with an extension and avoid the opponent's attempt to parry or press the blade, using as small a circular motion as possible. Circle under the opponent's blade. The first extension must be a believable feint in order to draw a reaction. Be prepared to proceed forward with a straight attack if no parry response is forthcoming.

Engagement

During an encounter between two fencers, the point at which the fencers are close enough to join blades, or to make an effective attack. Blade contact is also referred to as an engagement, whether just standing there, during a parry, attaque au fer, or prise de fer.

En garde

Spoken at outset to alert fencers to take defensive positions.

Feint

An offensive movement resembling an attack in all but its continuance. It is an attack into one line with the intention of switching to another line before the attack is completed. A feint is intended to draw a reaction from an opponent. This is the 'intention', and the reaction is generally a parry, which can then be deceived.

Parry

A simple defensive action designed to deflect an attack, performed with the forte of the blade. A parry is usually only wide enough to allow the attacker's blade to just miss; any additional motion is wasteful. A well-executed parry should take the foible of the attacker's blade with the forte and/or guard of the defender's. This provides the greatest control over the opponent's blade. Parries generally cover one of the 'lines' of the body. The simplest parries move the blade in a straight line. Other parries move the blade in a circular, semicircular, or diagonal manner.

It should be noted that Sebastian is a fictional character and that while the 6th Earl had ten children none were called Sebastian.

Glossary of sailing terms used in this book

Beam – The **beam** of a ship is its width at its widest point

Bowsprit – a spar projecting from the bow of a vessel, especially a sailing vessel, used to carry the headstay as far forward as possible.

Cable – A cable length or length of cable is a nautical unit of measure equal to one tenth of a nautical mile or approximately 100 fathoms. Owing to anachronisms and varying techniques of measurement, a cable length can be anywhere from 169 to 220 metres, depending on the standard used. In this book we assume 200 yards.

Cay – a low bank or reef of coral, rock, or sand especially one on the islands in Spanish America.

Futtock shrouds – are rope, wire or chain links in the rigging of a traditional square-rigged ship. They run from the outer edges of a top downwards and inwards to a point on the mast or lower shrouds, and carry the load of the shrouds that rise from the edge of the top. This prevents any tendency of the top itself to tilt relative to the mast.

Gripe – to tend to come up into the wind in spite of the helm.

Ketch – a two-masted sailing vessel, fore-and-aft rigged with a tall mainmast and a mizzen stepped forward of the rudderpost.

Knee – is a natural or cut, curved piece of wood.[1] Knees, sometimes called ships knees, are a common form of bracing in boatbuilding.

Knot – the measure of speed at sea. 1 knot = 1.11 miles.

Leeway – the leeward drift of a ship i.e. with the wind towards the lee side.

Loblolly boys – Surgeon's assistants

Lugger – a sailing vessel defined by its rig using the lug sail on all of its one or several masts. They were widely used as working craft, particularly off the coast. Luggers varied extensively in size and design. Many were undecked, open boats. Others were fully decked.

Mizzen – **1.** on a yawl, ketch or dandy the after mast.

          2. (on a vessel with three or more masts) the third mast from the bow.

Pawls – a catch that drops into the teeth of a capstan to stop it being pulled in reverse.

In ordinary – vessels "in ordinary" (from the 17th century) are those out of service for repair or maintenance, a meaning coming over time to cover a reserve fleet or "mothballed" ships.

Ratlines – are lengths of thin line tied between the shrouds of a sailing ship to form a ladder. Found on all square-rigged ships, whose crews must go aloft to stow the square sails, they also appear on larger fore-and-aft rigged vessels to aid in repairs aloft or conduct a lookout from above.

Rib – a thin strip of pliable timber laid athwarts inside a hull from inwale to inwale at regular close intervals to reinforce its planking. Ribs differ from frames or futtocks in being far smaller dimensions and bent in place compared to frames or futtocks, which are normally sawn to shape, or natural crooks that are shaped to fit with an adze, axe or chisel.

Sea anchor – any device, such as a bucket or canvas funnel, dragged in the water to keep a vessel heading into the wind or reduce drifting.

Shrouds – on a sailing boat, the shrouds are pieces of standing rigging which hold the mast up from side to side. There is frequently more than one shroud on each side of the boat. Usually, a shroud will connect at the top of the mast, and additional shrouds might connect partway down the mast, depending on the design of the boat. Shrouds terminate at their bottom ends at the chain plates, which are tied into the hull. They are sometimes held outboard by channels, a ledge that keeps the shrouds clear of the gunwales.

Stay – is part of the standing RIGGING and is used to support the weight of a mast. It is a large strong rope extending from the upper end of each mast.

Sweeps – another name for oars.

Tack – if a sailing ship is tacking or if the people in it tack it, it is sailing towards a particular point in a series of lateral movements rather than in a direct line.

Tumblehome – a hull which grows narrower above the waterline than its beam.

Wear ship – to change the tack of a sailing vessel, especially a square-rigger, by coming about so that the wind passes astern.

Weather Gauge – sometimes spelled weather gage is the advantageous position of a fighting sailing vessel relative to another. It is also known as "nautical gauge" as it is related to the sea shore.

If you have any questions, complaints or suggestions:

Please visit my website: www.thedorsetboy.com where you can leave a message or subscribe to the newsletter.

Or like and follow my Facebook page:

https://www.facebook.com/thedorsetboy

Or I can be found on twitter @ChristoperCTu3

Books by Christopher C Tubbs

The Dorset Boy Series.
A Talent for Trouble
The Special Operations Flotilla
Agent Provocateur
In Dangerous Company
The Tempest
Vendetta
The Trojan Horse
La Licorne
Raider
Silverthorn
Exile
Dynasty
Empire
Revolution

The Dorset Boy Lady Bethany Series
Graduation

The Scarlet Fox Series
Scarlett
A Kind of Freedom
Legacy

The Charlamagne Griffon Chronicles
Buddha's Fist

The Pharoah's Mask
Treasure of the Serpent God
The Knights Templar

See them all at:

Website: www.thedorsetboy.com
Twitter: @ChristoherCTu3
Facebook: https://www.facebook.com/thedorsetboy/
YouTube: https://youtu.be/KCBR4ITqDi4

Published in E-Book, Paperback and Audio formats on Amazon, Audible and iTunes

Printed in Great Britain
by Amazon

39298337R00209